## Swept Along in a River Full of Bad Ideas

Tansy closed her eyes for a second, running down the reasons this was *not* good enough, not one bit of it.

She was trying to keep her fool self out of trouble, not rush headlong into it.

Of all the rotten choices she'd made in a life too full of them, crossing the line into thieving was one mistake she'd never dared.

She'd hoped to stay put for a while in a place she knew well and try to catch her breath, not get caught up in some kind of harebrained caper and end up moving on in a hurry. Again.

And still...

Tansy wouldn't have to be the one doing the actual stealing, not with Cat already raring to go. And it wasn't like anyone would see them—or even hear them—if Tansy did the bang job right and Cat did her share and whipped up a nice distraction.

And she knew they both would.

Her brain was already lit up like the Fourth of July with ideas of how to do all that and more.

**The Great Gold Record Heist**

Copyright © 2025 by Kari A. Kilgore

All rights reserved

Published 2025 by Spiral Publishing, Ltd.
www.SpiralPublishing.net

Book and cover design copyright © 2025 by Spiral Publishing, Ltd.

Cover art copyright © 2025 by grandeduc | depositphotos.com

ISBN-13: 978-1-63992-040-2
Digital ISBN-13: 978-1-63992-041-9
Large Print ISBN-13: 978-1-63992-042-6
Hardcover ISBN-13: 978-1-63992-043-3

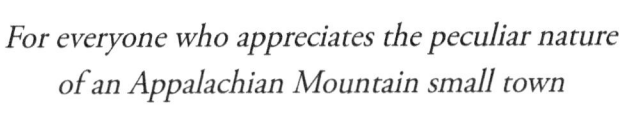

*For everyone who appreciates the peculiar nature*
*of an Appalachian Mountain small town*

# THE GREAT GOLD RECORD HEIST

KARI KILGORE

SPIRAL PUBLISHING, LTD.

# CHAPTER 1

ON A BEAUTIFUL MAY day down by the Clinch River, Tansy Stidham couldn't help but wonder why on earth she'd stayed away from home so long.

The river itself ran high and choppy from April's flood rains, with muddy brown water full of swirling whitecaps straining at the rocky banks as it rushed itself by in a great big hurry. Above all that water splashing and muttering to itself, the hillside rose up sharp and covered with a thick mess of trees putting on their best green finery to welcome the summer back home.

That sharp muddy-water smell on the cool spring breeze brought Tansy all the way back too, lifting her fine blonde hair away from her sweaty neck and filling her head full of home-sick memories.

Like a bunch of dumb teenage kids floating downstream in a country-kid-special raft of huge black inner tubes lashed together with rope they'd "borrowed" from someone's garage.

Feet and ass-ends cooled by the much slower water, while their arms, legs, and faces got scorched by Appalachian summertime sun.

On a blazing hot day—say up sometime in August—that old rubber itself could burn unlucky body parts just about as bad as the sun itself.

One of the tubes in the middle always held the cheap Styrofoam cooler full of ice and soda, and beer if they could find someone to buy it for them, which was most of the time. That cooler would get wrapped up like a mummy with all the rope that was left even though the damn thing could float all by itself.

Last thing anyone wanted on a big tubing party day was to have the cooler get away from them, or tip over and dump their refreshments before they had a chance to enjoy them.

Tansy doubted very much that tubing was even allowed on the river anymore, what with the new state park going in and all. Not that any tight-ass parent nowadays would ever let their precious offspring out the door without knowing where they were at all times, watched by smartphone and GPS and probably some kind of tracking tag they got shot up with the day the doctor smacked them on the backside.

Today she sat her own bony backside on a picnic table so new it still smelled of pine rather than hanging it down in the river. And her beverage of choice was a bottle of water from the cheapest gas station and main gossip hub just across the highway in Craigen.

Well, maybe not her beverage of *choice*, truth be told.

But the laws of the fair Commonwealth of Virginia had long ago convinced her to stay far, far away from the hard stuff when she got behind the wheel of whatever heap she drove.

Even with the painful help she'd had learning that lesson, Tansy had to admit it was one of the easiest ones she'd learned over the years. Or at least one she *kept* learned instead of backing herself right back up to the beginning more often than not.

The picnic table was one of several gathered on a huge gravel rectangle right down by the water, and not far off from where the Clinch took a sharp curve past downtown through a steep wall of gray rocks too straight and regular to be natural. Tansy had seen photographs of the big flood back in 1977, the worst anyone knew about for over a hundred years.

The whole town and several more in their mountainous region had damn near washed away that time instead of only leaving locals digging out from the usual floods on roadways back along the creeks and branches. A disaster bad enough that the river's current channel had been blasted clear out of the bedrock and a bunch of streets and such moved out of its original angry path.

Her own father had worked on that blasting crew, and told her stories from the time she was old enough to understand until the day his own bad habits took him out. He'd taught her everything he knew about blasting from that and years working in a coal mine, too, and never mind that she was a girl.

He'd also bragged to anyone who'd listen that his Tansy could wriggle herself into the smallest crack in any rock wall under or above the ground. When it came time for the big booms, she could work that rock like a surgeon, even better than he did.

And her Daddy was one of the best.

The result of all that excitement in town (and explosions Tansy dearly wished she'd seen for herself) was a lot less worry about a serious flood like that ever showing up again, at least so far about four decades later. And with that kind of stable waterway and the evaporation of regular jobs in the coal mines and timber industries, the Clinch River was ready for its starring role in the sparkling new tourism economy everyone kept carrying on about.

Tansy tipped her bottle back to finish her water, and crushed the plastic like she'd seen most of her family do every time they finished a beer. She screwed the red lid back on, took aim, and tossed it toward one of the big square wooden trashcans situated in a row beside the tables.

Her bottle caught on the blue plastic bag inside and flipped itself end over end onto the freshly trimmed grass outside the gravel. She snorted and got to her feet, brushing her faded jeans to make sure those tables weren't new enough to get gobs of sticky sap all over her.

"Best go fetch that bottle," a woman's drawling voice said from behind her. "They got big swarms of trash police around here these days just waiting to write up a bunch of fat tickets. Tickets for *throwing* trash like you just did, I should say. Not for *being* trash. Else the likes of me and you wouldn't be out walking around free."

The woman had somehow moved quiet as a stalking cat across the gravels before sitting herself down at another picnic table. Her cap of brown hair had curls too regular and unnatural to be anything but a perm, though Tansy had no idea where she'd dug one of those up.

4

She had a tan that looked every bit as fake as the curls to go with a faded Aerosmith t-shirt from at least twenty years ago.

And a smartass smirk that looked so familiar...

"Did you happen to go to high school here? And did I understand you meaning to say *I'd* go to jail if they decided to round up trash?"

The woman's narrow face held steady and serious for a few seconds, then a big grin cracked the memory vault in Tansy's head wide open.

"Hell yeah I went to high school here, and graduated same year as you, Tansy Stidham. Or maybe you go by some man or other's name these days, but that don't change who you are inside. And unless you've done a pure one-eighty on your general attitude towards life, I'd say the trash police might pick you up just to be on the safe side."

Tansy shook her head and didn't bother trying to fight back a grin of her own.

She hadn't let hardly anyone know she was back in town besides a couple of cousins who'd been part of their regular party circuit.

But however it happened, she was glad to see this ghost from her less-than-strictly-legal youth.

"That's Catrina Maybell," she said, "big as life and twice as bitchy. Unless *you* found some poor sap to walk you down the marrying plank, a trap I'm proud to say I've successfully avoided. Out of everyone still hanging around this little dead-end town, what the hell are the odds I'd run across you first time I come back in fifteen years?"

"That's Cat to anyone who knew me back in those days, especially ones who were foolish enough to run with the same backwards crowd." Cat stood and walked over to Tansy's table, still with that eerie silent motion even on tiny gravel that made all kinds of noise if something as light as a sparrow stepped on it. "I'd say you ought to run right out to town and play the lottery with luck running as good as yours, crossing paths with me. Where you been keeping yourself all this time?"

Tansy stood with her hands on her hips for a few seconds, shaking her head at the strange turn of events she didn't mind one tiny bit. She'd been pretty good friends with Cat back in school, and for the couple of years she'd lingered around Craigen before lighting out to look for greener pastures she never quite found.

More importantly, she'd seen and done enough when both of them were dumb kids—indeed running in the same back-wards crowd—to know all the odds about Cat Maybell that mattered.

As in about a million to one that she'd turned into some kind of snoop, or snitch, or worse, a straight-laced, uptight, and productive member of society.

About the same course her own life had taken, to say it right out rough and plain.

"You know how it is," Tansy said, sitting back down as Cat did the same. "Headed up to Cincinnati for a while, then out to Louisville, and lately all the way down to Atlanta. Every one of them turned out to have the same kinds of jobs that keep me running barely ahead of my bills without ever gaining a single step up on that success ladder we all keep hearing about. I never was the kind to think of college, but I took on some trade and technical school here and there."

All of that was true. But she'd left out several *very* well-paying jobs with highway departments and such on blasting crews. She'd tried her hand at building demolition a time or two, but she never quite developed the skill with taking down a structure—or the satisfaction—of bending rock to her will.

Not that the jobs or all that money had lasted long either, not with some of the questionable habits she was forever swearing to leave behind.

She sighed and waved her arm toward the small town hidden behind the human-carved bed of the Clinch.

"All *that* to say I figured I might pay a visit back home and see how that goes, so here I am about the same as when I started out. Just with a pile of aches and pains, a few more lines on my face, and more gray than I'd like trying to make itself a home in my hair. You?"

Cat pursed her lips and rolled her eyes exactly the same way she had as a teenager, usually when some other teenager did or said something too silly or crazy or dangerous for even another one known to take stupid chances to ignore.

Pretty impressive opinion coming from a confirmed firebug who'd worked out how to stay just under the arson radar, at least back then. Even if she was thinking about the most fearless—and somehow freakishly skilled and lucky—high-speed driver she'd ever come across.

"Wish I could say I was that well-traveled is all," Cat said. "Mainly been kicking around here and finding about the same thing as you did. Not hardly any way to keep up, much less manage to get ahead no matter how much you scrape and fight and struggle. I hear folks saying that's just the way it is and I need to cool my engines and get used to it. That never was my way to do things, though."

Tansy thought about asking what Cat meant by that last bit, but the defiant, challenging stare kept her from it.

Mainly because she kinda wanted in on whatever made Cat look that way.

"Then tell me what all has changed around here since I left," Tansy said. "I haven't even been into town past the Drop In and Shop yet, just sitting out here by myself thinking about nothing much until you showed up."

"Well, that's about what's changed, except you got to watch your ass a lot more if you dare creep a few miles over the slow-poke speed limit these days. Cops around every corner with a damn speed trap. Unless you count the new country music museum that went in a few months back. I guess that's a big deal to some that care about such things."

Tansy leaned forward, elbows on the bright yellow boards of the picnic table. It didn't quite have the gummy texture of fresh sap, but it had a faint stickiness she didn't like to think about.

"A museum? What, that Crooked Road music trail thing I keep seeing signs for? I had no idea it went through here. Who'd they dig up to be part of that? I thought all the real action was over in Bristol and out at the Carter Fold."

Cat nodded and rapped her reddened knuckles on the table.

"Sure, that's where all the *big* names are. But we have a bragging right or two here in Craigen and Vail County. Ever heard of Captain O'Quinn and the Confederates?"

Tansy thought for a second, her mind sorting through the town dump of her memories.

"They had some kind of big song in the 1970s, right? Something about a heartbreak as big as a mountain?"

"That's the very ones. Figured you'd know about it. Had a pretty big hit with that one, got them onto the national touring circuit with bigger acts a few times on account of how much other musicians love them even if they never sold all that well otherwise. Anyways, that's kind of what got the whole museum idea started. Gathering up their instruments and gear, music notebooks, that kind of thing. Brought in a whole mess of donations, some all the way from Nashville."

Tansy raised her eyebrows, wishing she'd driven down the main drag in Craigen for a look around instead of heading straight out here.

"Where'd they manage to put this museum? I wouldn't think anywhere in town would be big enough."

"They put it out on the edge of town, pretty as you please, near a bunch of new hiking and ATV trails. Damn babysitters will run you out for speeding there too, of course. Museum's in that old Vance place that got so run down after he got run out of town on the kind of charges no one will admit to knowing about, but put him on one of those federal registry lists for life. Not too far from the entrance to the Boody #3 Mine you might have heard about."

"I remember that place," Tansy said. "The house, not the mine. Nice enough probably fifty years ago, but it was a mess by the time we were in high school. I sure remember that old asshole leering at all of us. Who put up the cash for all that work?"

Cat rolled her hand in a circle and ended up pointing it like a gun at Tansy's chest.

"*That's* the real question, ain't it? Whatever the town council did to get all this pulled together is still locked up too tight for the gossip vultures to get hold of it. I do know Captain O'Quinn's widow was neck deep in making it happen. Word is she was happy to get rid of most of his stuff, especially if her name went on a plaque or two and got written up in the papers again. From what I hear, they have enough crammed in there that the stuff is worth more than the house will ever be."

Cat tilted her head to the side and gave Tansy an odd, curious look.

"You don't remember the old Boody Mine? What happened there after it shut down?"

# CHAPTER 2

TANSY SCOWLED, trying to dig out the faint tickle of memory so she could catch hold of it.

Something about...growing something?

Or stealing electricity, maybe?

That *couldn't* be right.

"I'm sure I have this wrong, because it was after I moved away and I probably heard it third- or fourth-hand. Did someone get caught tapping into the electrical lines?"

Cat grinned again and smacked the table.

"That's just exactly what happened, at least what got them caught. See, a bunch of coal miners who quit pretending like they weren't permanently out of a job decided to move into that old abandoned mine and set up an operation of their own. Only they didn't aim to dig coal. They had the nicest pot-growing setup you ever did see."

Tansy laughed and nodded.

"*Now* I remember. They shorted out a circuit, right?

Otherwise they might still be down there with a row of grow-lights today."

"Probably so," Cat said. "What with Virginia getting on board the legal pot train, they might do well to set that whole thing up again instead of fussing with building greenhouses. Keeping common thieves out would be a hell of a lot easier too. Listen, did you know my Uncle Casey was part of all that mess?"

Tansy shook her head, not sure whether to smile or not.

"I'm real sorry to hear that, Cat. I hope he didn't get into too much trouble."

"Nowhere near what that asshole deserved. What I'm getting at is he had all the maps of that old mine and all the land around it laying around his house for years. Might be those maps disappeared not long before they got themselves caught. Might also be my jerk of an uncle never noticed the maps had walked themselves off."

Tansy sat back, taking another look at Cat. Not at all sure whether she was trustworthy now, even though they each knew enough about the other's potentially criminal hobbies to keep them a good bit more honest.

And not sure she cared one way or the other about that, if this conversation kept getting more interesting.

Being damn near broke with pitiful prospects at her age wasn't what anyone with two brain cells left to jam together would call fun.

"What are you getting at?" she said. "If you've got those maps, or blueprints, or whatever they are, why are you telling me?"

Cat nodded once, with a strangely satisfied expression.

"Well, like you said, jobs you can get without a fancy college degree or two never seem to deliver on that promise of making a difference in people's lives. Not people like us, leastways. I'm telling you because I might have happened to notice how those old mine shafts go right under parts of Craigen. Might even sneak under that new museum."

Tansy let out a breathy "huh" before she could stop herself, and not entirely because she was surprised.

This was the most excited she'd felt in years, about anything.

"Are you saying you think you can steal things out of that museum, Cat? Right through a mine shaft?"

Cat shrugged and her thin lips turned down in a frown.

"I'm not saying much of anything about all of that. Just catching up with an old friend, right? Thing is, the stuff in that museum is worth an awful lot of money to the right kind of people. The best part is how many of them already perked up and begged to get their chance at the haul."

Tansy brushed her hair back, then scrubbed her fingertips against her scalp.

"What, all that stuff from Nashville? Don't they have it locked up or guarded or something?"

Cat smiled and tapped her temple.

"Now that would draw all kinds of attention to itself, wouldn't it? If some kind of exclusive, one-of-a-kind treasure on loan from a *real* country music star up and walked out of here? I'd have to guess no one anywhere within a thousand miles would be willing to buy whatever might happen to end up on the market. Not anything so *well-known* as all that."

"Then you're thinking about the stuff that isn't so famous."

A slow smile worked across Tansy's face. "Like maybe the Captain O'Quinn stuff. Hardly anyone outside of this little town knows about most of it these days, and a bunch of them are too young to remember. And I'd bet a whole bunch of local folks would like to get their hands on it. The kinds of folks who'd be a hell of a lot more likely to pony up the cash and keep their mouths shut to make sure they don't get into trouble themselves."

Cat held up both hands and shrugged.

"Folks like us, more or less. No one's ever said I'm any kind of an expert, but I'm not half bad at seeing when someone's lit up by an idea. I see that on your face right now. So right now's the time to come clean and tell me if I'm seeing wrong. Tell you the truth, I been trying to figure out how to get into that museum after closing time since it opened. Now I think I see how we might actually pull it off."

Tansy sighed, wishing she had a big, healthy shot of the hard stuff she wasn't willing to drive with. Maybe from one of the suppliers she'd heard about from her grandparents years ago, hidden far enough back on a ridge somewhere that someone had to tell you the way before you could find them. Better yet, show you the way themselves.

And even then, you better make damn sure the producers of such fine under-the-taxation-radar beverages knew you were on the way if you didn't want to get greeted with the barrel of a shotgun.

"I'm not going to tell you anything right now, one way or the other," she said. "But I am going to ask you a question you can decide on your own whether you want to answer or not.

You didn't just *happen* to wander down this way and just *happen* to run into me today, did you?"

Cat didn't stare at her or hesitate or pretend to be confused or even surprised. That by itself went a long way toward convincing Tansy to stay right where she was and listen.

After all, she'd gotten involved in schemes a lot less sensible with a lot less chance of reward with a hell of a lot less chance of success, and with much less trustworthy characters than Cat Maybell.

"Of course I didn't just wander down here," Cat said, "with no more expectation than getting yet another look at the same muddy river or catching a random litterbug stranger, as if I give a damn about the trash police. You probably don't know your cousins are more tickled than a pig in shit for your visit, Tansy. Word gets around like a lightning strike in a small town that happens to include text messaging in every busybody's pockets thanks to the new cellphone tower they all voted against."

"Sure, that's fair. Even though I can't say I'm planning to see more than a couple of them. The rest are either batshit crazy or meaner than I've ever pretended to be. But that doesn't explain how you knew I'd be right here."

Cat shook her head and smiled.

"Know exactly what you mean about the kinfolk, and no amount of sugar or moonshine will help that truth go down. I'd just as soon jump into that trashcan myself and tell you to roll me down into the river than spend time with most of 'em. Not without they was in handcuffs and behind bars for good measure."

She pulled a huge smartphone out of her back pocket, a brand-new top-of-the-line model from what Tansy could tell.

Not exactly what a self-proclaimed broke single woman getting by on jobs she could scrape together might be expected to have.

"That's where the modern age that's finally bothered itself to arrive in Craigen comes in right damn handy. I put the word out to a few folks that I hoped to see you while you were in town. Especially a couple of our old high school buddies who work at that fine convenience store right there off the highway. You'd be surprised how much of the whole county's news and gossip passes right through those doors. Got the note that you showed up to buy that water that you so unkindly chucked onto the grass, so I headed out the door."

Tansy had no doubt who Cat had talked to at The Drop In and Shop, and even less that they'd been happy to spread the incredibly exciting news that someone long gone had drifted in off the springtime breeze. It had to be Tim Calloway and Mark Morris. They'd been best friends—and first-rate chatterboxes and rumor-spreaders—since they and Tansy and Cat were all in grade school together.

And people always said *women* were the ones who loved to talk about everyone else's business.

"They said I'd be down here? Not sure I'm gonna buy that, not if you plan for us to work together."

Now Cat's nod and smile were approving and sneaky at the same time.

"Not that many Georgia license plates around by the river in the middle of the week, so you were easy enough to spot. I checked out three other picnic spots before I saw you. If I hadn't struck lucky here, I would have started asking around."

Tansy stared at her. "Keep going."

"As far as why *you* before you get around to asking about *that*, I couldn't hardly forget how good you were with making things go boom. Not between you demonstrating a time or three and your Daddy bragging about you from dawn to dusk. Hearing your name sparked off the whole idea in my noggin. I think we'd make a damn fine team. That enough information for this line of work?"

Tansy closed her eyes for a second, running down the reasons this was *not* good enough, not one bit of it.

She was trying to keep her fool self out of trouble, not rush headlong into it.

Of all the rotten choices she'd made in a life too full of them, crossing the line into thieving was one mistake she'd never dared.

She'd hoped to stay put for a while in a place she knew well and try to catch her breath, not get caught up in some kind of harebrained caper and end up moving on in a hurry. Again.

And still...

If the kindly Widow O'Quinn had been so eager to part with all her man's stuff, she wouldn't likely mind too much if it all disappeared. And if she did, surely the offer of a nice, juicy reward from Captain O'Quinn and the Confederates money from all those tours and record sales would fetch it back right quick. The museum had to carry some kind of insurance, too.

Tansy wouldn't have to be the one doing the actual stealing, not with Cat already raring to go. And it wasn't like anyone would see them—or even hear them—if Tansy did the bang job right and Cat did her share and whipped up a nice distraction.

And she knew they both would.

Her brain was already lit up like the Fourth of July with ideas of how to do all that and more.

She wouldn't even have to do the selling, which probably had a lot higher odds of getting someone in trouble. Sounded like Cat had that part all wrapped up. With Cat's gift of running her mouth and convincing people to go along with her crazy stunts and plans, Tansy figured that was the truth.

Most important, and the thing she was least likely to put up much of a fight against?

Tansy couldn't bring the last time she was this stirred up about much of anything to mind no matter how hard she tried.

The last time she felt that tingle of excitement in the depths of her belly, or the electric sparks that charged from her head to her toes and everywhere in between.

It would take a towering pile of reasons *against* to make up for that one last powerful reason *for.*

Tansy opened her eyes and smiled. Then she lied through her teeth.

Because she was about a thousand miles past talk and picking up speed along the slippery-slide express road to action.

"All right, I'm curious enough to at least hear you out, maybe get a look at those maps of yours. But I'm not promising anything. And if you already put the word out to so many buyers that the local cops are keeping a close watch on the place, this is over before it ever starts. Understand?"

Cat kept her expression calm, but those same flashes of thrill-lightning were blasting off in her eyes.

"Understand, and right glad to hear it. One thing I can guaran-damn-tee is the word isn't out to anyone besides me and you. Not about the details of how and when it might go down. Last thing I'd want to do is get even one extra set of eyes on that museum, and you can take *that* to the bank. But when it comes to finding suckers to take all that garage-sale music junk off our hands, just leave that to me. Won't take more than a day or two."

Cat finally grinned. "I still say you ought to run and get yourself a stack of lottery tickets, Tansy Stidham. Cause this *damn* sure is a lucky day for both of us."

# CHAPTER 3

Tansy never would have considered herself a patron of any kind of art, not unless you counted her own under-appreciated skill at slicing through rock the way most folks might wish they could carve pie, or cake, or meat.

But she had to admit she was surprised and impressed at how nice the Country on the Clinch Music Museum and Gallery was set up and put together.

Whoever did the restoration on the old Vance place could take on high-end contracts down in Atlanta for rich white folks buying up houses in old neighborhoods and forcing out all the locals, for one thing.

The once-filthy and mossy stone walls looked maintained instead of blasted too bright and clean and new, and all the dingy or broken windows and forest-green trim were in good repair for the first time she could remember.

They'd built on a proper wraparound sitting porch to replace the cramped stoop the creepy old man used to perch on like a vulture, with a row of rocking chairs painted the same purple and gold as the high school's Deacons mascot.

No one rocked on an early morning that turned out overcast, chilly, and cool, like the year decided May was a bad idea after all and reversed itself to jump back into March instead.

She'd made one of her usual snap decisions and accepted Cat's invitation to stay the night at her place, not too hard after they'd spent the whole rest of the previous day and evening running their mouths about The Great and Changeable Plan.

Cat wanted to call it The Perfect Plan, but Tansy shut that bullshit down before Cat even got rolling with it. Tansy was no genius, but she knew plans had a funny way of blowing up in your face like a fast-fuse charge if you decided you'd thought of everything.

And not a nice, pretty, controlled blast either. This was likely to be the kind that shattered the thing you were trying so hard to protect and exploded everything else into dust.

It's like whoever (or whatever) drives all the machines behind the scenes of life hears a person say that word *perfect*, or even think it, and starts giggling with one hand full of sugar and the other full of sand to sprinkle into the gears until they gum plumb up.

So they'd sat on the cheap-but-clean brown furniture in Cat's near-empty white-walled apartment, contenting themselves with a couple of beers rather than moving on to the hard stuff because Tansy refused to say a word otherwise. And they'd talked and jawed and yammered until her throat felt almost as sore and tender as if she'd landed herself with a bad case of strep throat.

Staring at faded mining maps so old they'd been folded

through in spots, comparing them with newer plots of the whole of Craigen and downloaded layouts of the museum last of all turned out to be more fun than she imagined.

But that could only take them so far despite all those words and sketches and notes scribbled in a rusty spiral notebook.

So seeing the museum for herself was the only thing that made any kind of sense.

*By* herself, too, a point Cat hadn't much bothered to argue about. Not once Tansy pointed out no one at the museum would be likely to recognize or remember her since they'd only opened a couple of years back.

Cat then managed to further improve her reliability score by admitting she'd been in there too many times already checking the place out. And by predicting the museum would be empty that time of day, which turned out to be true.

A young man trying *way* too hard to act local met Tansy at the door, and proceeded to tell her all about the history of her own damn hometown while they strolled through the transformed house. His purple t-shirt featured the same logo of a banjo with rolling mountains across the round part that was plastered all over signs in town and on a pile of cheap junk for sale in one corner.

Tansy pretended to be surprised and excited by how much he knew about Craigen and Vail County and the coalfields in general, and made a show of peering at all the huge shiny glass cases along the floor and thick frames hung all over the carefully tan walls.

In her own opinion, she did a fine job of playing like she was mightily impressed with a bunch of wrinkled showbills, vinyl albums and singles, and truly horrible costumes from touring acts of decades thankfully gone by. She'd swear the stink of stale cigarettes, booze, and greasy road food drifted its way out of those cases even though the air conditioning was set a little bit below the beer-chilling zone despite the chilly day.

She even tapped her foot and nodded along to what most people visiting the museum would probably call great music, but had *way* too many banjos and fiddles and screechy wailing for her taste.

She couldn't get down to the real business of the visit until Mr.    Oh-How-I-Love-This-Dear-Quaint-Little-Town    got distracted by a tour bus rolling into view, apologized as if he'd just stranded her in a white dress at the altar, and *finally* left her alone.

Again, right on schedule from Cat's sneaky peek at the list of when groups were expected.

The one room Tansy was actually interested in was toward the back, with a window overlooking the carefully manicured back yard with flowerboxes going right along the tree line, complete with a firepit and a tiny little stage for live music.

From the room's long, rectangular shape and a floor that felt like tile under the smooth gold rug, it was probably the kitchen back when people lived there instead of a collection of stuff owned by the dead.

And every inch was given over to make a weird shrine to none other than Captain O'Quinn and the Confederates and their questionable contribution to country and bluegrass music history.

These displays were upgraded to include guitars, banjos, and mandolins, alongside drums, cymbals, and tambourines, all in various states from sparkly and brand-new to dull, cracked, or punched right through.

A bunch of original songs scribbled on lined notebook paper, scraps of the dingy white backs of ripped up tour posters, and yes, even the fabled napkins were tucked in between the rest. Someone had even donated a thick stack of very old-fashioned printed concert ticket stubs, from smudgy bits that looked like old raffle tickets to the most recent versions with colorful borders and dates and venues.

Neither the Captain nor his Confederate buddies made it to the era of phone-based tickets that never did get printed (and made for rotten memorabilia).

But the holy grail for Tansy, Cat, and the collectors lurking back in these mountains like the moonshiners had to be the one and only gold record the band ever earned.

The simple wooden frame with black matte fabric inside hung at her eye-level, with a perfectly tasteful spotlight reflecting the gold disc inside. A quick internet search the night before told her it wasn't actually *made* of gold, and it might not even be a 45 of "Mountain Deep Heartache" at all, even though that's what the blue label on the record said. Nothing more than some ordinary vinyl record spray-painted to look like 24 carats.

An internet search she hadn't done where Cat could see it, and Tansy decided to keep that little bit of information all to herself just in case it came in handy someday.

The sentimental value would get her and Cat the reward for all this sneaking around in broad daylight. Someone, and probably a lot of someones, would want this fancy plaque saying at least half a million people had bought the proper single a long time ago.

That and whatever else they could manage to liberate from this cozy little room.

A general clatter and burst of voices warned her as passengers from the tour bus invaded the museum. Tansy took a quick second to glance around the walls and ceiling. A handful of security cameras, which would be easy enough for her and Cat to fool with the right clothes and a dead simple full-face mask. No sign of the telltale red gleam of more advanced security, and Cat said she hadn't seen any kind of monitors besides one laptop on her peek into the museum's office.

Not that Tansy expected that in such a small town, impressive display setup or not.

Sure, it was possible they had some kind of alert set up with the town cops or an outside security service or even the county sheriff's office over in Wise. But if the townies were anything like she remembered from her youthful hellraising days, they'd have a hell of a time even finding the museum, much less figuring out something as odd as a brand-new entrance in the basement.

Both of the more effective law enforcement options would take a good long while to get to Craigen unless they happened to be passing by.

Not that she'd seen hide nor hair of any kind of cop on her visit so far. Not in such a neighborly, friendly, *safe* little tourist town.

She thumped the heel of her sneaker against the floor.

Yep, that was tile, and way too much trouble to try to break through from the bottom.

She walked out of the shrine to a hit record that had surprised the band most of all, then turned toward the back of the house instead of toward the noisy group out front. Sure enough, a six-panel wooden door marked *Private* stood right where the old blueprints said it should.

The door to the basement, which would be a hell of a lot easier to get into, and out of, once she got some quality alone time in the abandoned mine much closer underfoot than anyone else seemed to remember.

She glanced toward the front again, pulling a wadded-up paper towel out of her back pocket. No sign of hinges on this side of the door, so it probably opened in toward the basement. She darted forward and tried to twist the shiny brass handle with the paper towel keeping her fingers and pesky prints away from the surface.

No movement in either direction, but neither the door nor the handle felt rock-solid, either. She could wiggle both a good bit, as if the brand-new hardware didn't quite sit right in the ancient, not-maintained-for-decades door.

Someone had scrubbed it up pretty, sure. But the run-down legacy of Creepy Old Man Vance lingered around the place like the oily stink of his unwashed hair and clothes.

Tansy waited for the chattery and giggly bunch to get themselves spread out nice and even through the rooms, then carefully avoided catching the tour guide's attention as she headed out. From the looks of their tailored clothes and fancy hairdos, they'd come from a bigger city to enjoy a tour of the charmingly rustic roots of country music, and more than a little bit of the roots of rock and roll.

So not a one of them would recognize her, or likely

remember one woman out of at least thirty people crowded inside.

Back out in the chilly, overcast day, Tansy let the smile she'd kept to herself come through.

This job was going to be tricky, sure. And a crazy number of things could still go wrong.

But her little tour of the Country on the Clinch Music Museum and Gallery had put a satisfying number of her fears to rest.

And cranked up her too-often-reckless excitement considerably.

# CHAPTER 4

GETTING into the old coal-mine-turned-pot-mine ended up a lot easier than Tansy expected, even after her years of exploring abandoned mines and every other kind of cave with her father.

And Cat's eerie ability to remain cool and steady while rocketing them there in a smelly old beater of a sedan gave Tansy yet another example of how some things back home never changed. Cat never flinched as she swerved around huge potholes and chunks of exposed rock as easy as breathing.

The original mine apparently dated from way back when Craigen was barely a smudge on anyone's map, long before the old Vance place was built. She had no idea what dumbass surveyor allowed any kind of building to go in so close above an old mine shaft.

It was a damn miracle and the luck of solid bedrock that there hadn't been any kind of sinkholes or other trouble in all that time.

The last mining company to operate out here—obviously

without competent engineering or honest inspections—had gone bankrupt in spectacular fashion when the scant easy-to-get coal dried up back in the 1970s. They'd left a towering stack of unpaid bills and a furious gang of support staff and unpaid miners behind.

What they hadn't bothered to do before they split town was properly secure the entrance, any more than they'd bothered to let anyone know the coal seam was getting close to tapped out before they even set up operations.

Not that any of that stopped them from hiring a bunch of people, knowing they'd only be able to fill one big, profitable order at most before they closed up shop and split town.

From what she'd read and how Cat told the tale, the pot mine turned a hell of a lot more profit while it was operating than the coal outfit ever did.

An overgrown, twisty gravel road that started out a couple of miles outside of Craigen before curving in close took her and Cat straight to a decrepit set of blue metal buildings. A couple had already collapsed into jagged piles of mostly rust.

But the one they needed was intact enough to get the job done.

It looked like nothing more than a storage shed built up against a steep, rocky slope, with scraggly poplar trees here and there putting on their brand-new leaves for the season poking up through a rotten mess of weeds and briars. Once Cat used an ordinary crowbar to liberate the door from its hinges (quickly and easily enough to leave Tansy impressed and a little nervous), they were staring down an impressive pile of broken tools and equipment rusted to junk and coated with black coal dust.

The remains of gardening supplies—like the shredded plastic bags of fertilizer, a pile of huge, broken fluorescent bulbs, and an honest-to-goodness rusty watering can—looked strangely out of place. A mess of thin, warped, yellow-pine two-by-fours and smaller bits didn't look like they could do much good in a coal mine, but Tansy figured they would have come in right handy for some kind of underhanded, underground gardener.

They'd be downright essential to part of her escape plan.

But most importantly, a hulking hole in the mountain itself seemed to absorb all the light from their bright headlamps.

"You *sure* this thing is safe?" Cat said. "Doubt anyone's been out here since they raided the dope operation and hauled what they could out for evidence. Not even teenagers bother with a place like this these days. Hardly any of them can handle the drive, and the rest are too damn lazy."

Tansy had tried to convince her to ride this one out at her apartment, but Cat got her back up and insisted on coming along. Now an already dangerous and difficult gig had the extra stress of worrying about an inexperienced person along.

One who could easily get hurt, or mess something up badly enough to get them both killed.

Not exactly the best way to get going on a new job.

"Not even a little bit sure it's safe," Tansy said. "I told you that, remember? When you still could have stayed back at your place and left me to this part? I won't stop you if you decide to park yourself right here while I go inside. If anyone can make this bang work, I will. I promise. You *sure* you haven't talked to anyone else about this whole idea? One of those jailbird cousins of yours, maybe?"

Cat snorted and shook her head, but her grin looked a little bit too big to Tansy.

"Like I told you yesterday, I can think of about a hundred unpleasant things I'd do before I'd talk to those assholes about anything. Much less something like this they could decide to use against me, and they would, too. Bet your ass they would. You talk to anyone else?"

Tansy shrugged. "Don't know when I would have. We went right to your apartment, remember? I haven't been anywhere else besides my little shopping trip for supplies. Before you pipe up and get all paranoid about it, yes, my dipshit cousin Vickie works out at the farm supply on her work-release program. But I didn't say one single word to her or get close to her. They've got her sweeping and mopping and cleaning up crap as far as I can tell, so all she could do was glare at me. My guess is she'll find some way to cheat her way out of the work, or maybe steal enough brooms and buckets to end up right back in jail."

Cat shivered and rubbed her arms.

"That's almost like she *knew* what you were about to get into. Vickie's the very reason *I* knew who Captain O'Quinn was most of my life, the way she carried on about her Daddy helping write 'Mountain Deep Heartache' and all. Claimed her Daddy had the idea for the band's name, even gave them their first tour bus and everything."

Tansy stared at Cat, but she wasn't seeing her at all. Her mind had abruptly yanked her back in time, to those strange childhood years when everyone assumed kids would always get along with their cousins and want to spend as much time as possible with them.

No matter how much they flat-out didn't like each other.

"Is *that* who she was talking about? I remember her running her mouth about her Daddy being right in the middle of something famous or important. A whole bunch of some-things, to tell you the truth. If Uncle Arn had been into even half the stuff she swore he was, he wouldn't have had the spare time to get up to making her or any of his other kids. I didn't half listen. Always figured it was bullshit."

"Oh, it was pure, top-of-the-line, Grade-A *certified* bull-shit." Cat rolled her eyes. "I guess I listened to her more than you did, probably 'cause I never got stuck at Thanksgiving and Christmas and every other holiday with her grouchy ass. Never did find one person to back up a single word she said."

"Just as well I didn't listen then," Tansy said. "Nothing but a bunch of smelly hot air in the end."

She didn't mention the way Vickie put a stranglehold on her mop and glowered the whole time Tansy walked the cramped aisles of the farm supply, pushing a tiny buggy with a gritty handle and one squeaky wheel. If that old saw about *if looks could kill* had the slightest whisper of truth, Tansy knew she'd be laid out on a slab over at the crooked funeral home over in Estonoa.

Rumor in the family and around town was Vickie had used more than a glare to kill, at least once. And tried to more times than that, but hadn't quite managed to make it work out.

She'd got it into her head a long time ago that one of the families who lived near their grandparents decided to buy the sprawling old Harbury place outside of town for no other reason at all but to stop Vickie from buying it. Neither Tansy, the neighbors, or anyone else ever saw evidence that Vickie so much as put in an offer on that house, and as far as Tansy knew, it sat there empty still.

Mainly because the neighbors had no desire to wonder when they might get an unwelcome visitor in the middle of the night.

Maybe only yelling and screeching.

Maybe armed.

Maybe carrying a lighter and a can of gasoline.

They moved to another county not long after that.

But Vickie never forgave them, and never tired of telling anyone who would listen how they'd done her wrong.

Cat shivered again and stared toward what looked like a passage into nothing at all. They'd stirred up enough dust walking in that specks danced across the paths of their lights, but not moving in any particular direction.

Dead air, in other words. No sign of another end to this mine.

At least not one that was open.

No off smells, thank goodness, not besides the musty shed and rancid motor oil. Not even a hint of the sweetish stink of dope lingered.

Cat finally blew out a breath, sending all those motes of dust swirling into patterns a lot like the busy currents in the Clinch River.

"I reckon I should have an idea how the whole thing works in the end," she said. "The faster we get the goods, the sooner the folks about ready to line up to take home a little piece of Captain O'Quinn and the Confederates of their very own will be happy to pay up. So we're better off working together. But you'll warn me before you blow anything up, right?"

Tansy couldn't resist shrugging.

"I'll do the best I can, you know that. Sometimes rocks dislodge themselves from the ceiling, especially in an old mine like this. Just look around this place. You think any mining outfit that ran this much on the cheap took extra-special care with keeping the roof safe and secure? And I have to say I highly doubt the dope growers worked according to any kind of safety standards."

Instead of shivering or complaining, or just walking back outside, Cat only stared into Tansy's eyes, then down the mine opening again. Tansy had to give her credit for showing that much courage.

"Well, I guess if you don't have yourself too scared to go inside with talk like that," Cat said, "it can't be near as dangerous as you say. Right? Come on, let's get it over with and get out of here."

Fighting back the urge to tell Cat anything that happened from here on out was her own stubborn damn fault, Tansy decided to be nice about it.

Within reason.

"Listen, you saw those old original maps. This mine was dug out a long time ago, way before the last money grubbers took over. The roof's been steady for decades, and no reports of gas building up that I could find, and you know the dope farmers sampled their own goods at some point. Probably never was enough coal for the methane to bother showing up. My guess is your pot growers got in quick as they could without digging out any new chambers, then scooted with the cash. Our biggest worry is making sure we don't blow the whole museum up trying to worm our way into that basement. Okay?"

Cat took a deep enough breath that her slight shoulders seemed to rise up near her ears.

"It's not far along, right? You said less than half a mile on account of how the road curved."

Tansy pulled out her phone and tapped the screen. She didn't have a trace of signal on this side of the mountain even before they went underground, but she'd downloaded everything they'd need.

"According to everything I could see, all we have to do is keep count of our steps and make one turn to the right. We do that part, and we'll be damn close to the prize. Grab a couple of those pine boards, would you? We'll need 'em later."

# CHAPTER 5

CAT YANKED her Army-green canvas bag onto her back when Tansy shifted her own much bigger backpack on her shoulders. They'd argued over the contents of their bags more than just about anything else, mainly about how much room they had to keep empty versus how many supplies they really needed.

In the end, they'd settled on less than Cat wanted, and more than Tansy did.

Tansy hadn't quite cleared everything with Cat, of course. The tools her Daddy taught her to never be without were tucked away inside. Including one the Commonwealth of Virginia wouldn't be happy she kept hidden without a concealed carry permit saying she could.

As far as she was concerned, the homemade explosives were a hell of a lot more dangerous than a regular handgun, so the Commonwealth could kiss her shiny pink backside, as her Daddy would have said.

Thank all the gods of a shared small-town childhood, she

and Cat hadn't disagreed one single time on what to wear on this little adventure.

Jeans still dark enough to blend at night, and old enough neither one cared if they ended up in a dumpster in the morning. Long-sleeved shirts in pretty much the same shape: tight around the wrists to stay put and maybe block out a little bit of the dust.

And cheap rain jackets bought the day before at the local crap shack.

Tansy doubted either one of them would stop a drop of rain, or even high humidity. And the dark gray color was likely to get anyone wearing one hit by a car if they were foolish enough to try to cross the street in bad weather.

But they'd do just fine for keeping two thieves hard to identify on a typical security camera.

Cat picked up two boards barely as wide as her skinny wrist and long as her arm, Tansy grabbed a short length of metal a little bit longer than the crowbar she'd stashed in the car, and they headed in.

As they walked, the evidence of this old mine's shutdown and rebirth as a marijuana growing hideout showed up in the clear, bright beams of their lights. Not much coal dust on the floor or walls, none on the roof to speak of. Only the rough edges of dingy gray rock and hardly any darker streaks at all.

A few traces of the grow-cave were still visible in long rectangular frames of wood the cops hadn't bothered hauling out, turning gray and falling apart all these years later. All the bootleg wiring and lights were gone, probably stored in some courthouse as evidence.

Everything Cat claimed and Tansy verified online seemed to be true so far.

And the determination to get this crazy scheme to work out somehow burned higher and hotter in Tansy's belly with every cautious step.

She'd opened a useful little app that let her tap the screen on her phone to count anything: one she'd used for any number of odd jobs or for work or to pass the damn time when nothing much else was going on. Right now, she needed to keep track of how far they'd gone to make sure they didn't wander off down some dead-end corridor under the ground.

Sure, they could get back out by retracing their steps, and a mine this old was likely to stay stable. But the last thing she wanted to do was set off a blast in the wrong place and miss their mark.

Or draw attention to the noise, or manage to get one or both of them hurt.

Cat kept walking closer and closer to her side, bumping into her or poking her with the boards, and withdrawing across the narrow passage. Between that and Cat's fast, gasping breath, Tansy was afraid she'd panic before they got anywhere near the promised half a mile.

And the rising stink of Cat's fearful sweat was a lot less pleasant than the musty underground air.

But Tansy finally saw the rounded tunnel curve a bit to the left, and another square-sided passage open on the right. What she didn't see was any trace of the pot miners and their clever operation. They'd never gotten big enough to need to expand this far back into the old mine.

Nothing here but a hole in the mountain abandoned a long time ago.

And exactly where it should be according to the number glowing blue on her screen. She leaned her metal bar against the wall so she wouldn't trip herself and block her own damn escape route.

"Okay, this is our turn," she said, not sure why she kept her voice so quiet. "I need you to hang back and let me work now, hear me? Otherwise I might end up getting nervous and take too many steps and punch a leak in the swimming pool instead and drown both our sorry asses."

Cat's wide-eyed stare had Tansy wondering if she'd gone too far with that one, which was scarier than Tansy wanted to admit. The pool was several blocks on toward town, and thankfully for all the kiddies that used it, a long way past any of these forgotten excavations.

Cat finally smacked her free hand over her own mouth to stifle a flurry of disturbingly little-girl giggles.

"Ohhhh sure, *that's* gonna happen to Virg Stidham's little girl. The way I remember it, and saw you do a few times, you'd be more likely to lose the way from the top of the head to your own ass. Don't you worry. You didn't fuss and quarrel over my driving, unlike most of the cowards around these parts. I'll keep my distance and let you operate."

Tansy turned away in case the relief swarming through her mind showed too clearly on her face, and tried to watch both the uneven floor covered with gravels and her phone's display at the same time.

Unless her stride had altered itself after being steady for decades—one of the many useful things Virg Stidham taught her that came in handy all the damn time—they were right under the museum's huge basement.

And she was faced with the most delicate blasting job of her life.

One her own Daddy might have balked at, given the chance.

But he'd passed on his stubbornness to his little girl in full measure, right along with his willingness to chase a great big thrill longer and harder than just about anyone else would.

Not the best trait when it came to settling down to live a useful and productive life.

A hell of a boring life as far as Tansy was concerned, no matter how many times she tried to convince herself otherwise.

She didn't need the phone to visualize how the two spaces overlapped each other: the stone chamber she stood inside and the basement barely five feet above her head.

She'd lined up the house blueprint with the old mine layout at least a dozen times the night before.

Enough so she could see each one of them in her mind, bright and clear and detailed enough to touch.

As long as she stayed to the middle of this hollowed-out box where a few dribbles of coal and a bunch of junk rock used to be, she'd be dead on her mark.

She swung her backpack off her shoulders and settled it to the uneven stone under her feet.

Time to get busy and make her Daddy proud, and do her level best to keep from sending herself and Cat straight to hell to join him.

Her quick little shopping trip before going to Cat's place for their planning/running-their-mouths session gave her everything she needed to make the shaped charge after Cat fell asleep. Nothing more than the same old mix of ingredients she'd learned when her hair was still in pigtails.

Some from the grocery store, some from the farm supply.

Stuff most folks would never think twice about.

A few things she got hold of carefully and always kept with her, because hardly anyone thought about them at all. But if people who knew half as much as she did saw her buying them, they'd bring a whole lot more suspicion and questions than Tansy cared to deal with.

The final result now set up nice and neat in a cone she'd measured out in her mind and on paper over and over again before she ever put her hands on the real thing.

Now it was just a matter of finding the right divot in the gray stone about a foot over her head, setting the charge, and hauling her ass back to where Cat waited in the other chamber.

Smooth and easy, no troubles for even her busy little mind to hang onto, as Daddy would have said.

That was one of his nuggets of wisdom Tansy had long ago dismissed as bullshit. But she got on with it anyway.

Charge tucked into a jagged little crevice and ready to go, she grabbed her pack with one hand and spun the tiny wheel on a cheap plastic lighter with the other.

She knew very well how to use a high-tech detonator with countdowns and sparks and safeties and all. Every legit job she'd had with highway departments and building droppers and such had insisted on modern technology.

Fair enough with so many other people and buildings and roads around, she supposed.

When it came to her own work—especially an extremely

private gig like this one—nothing suited her better than a plain old-fashioned length of corded fuse.

One more glance around, and she leaned up and touched the lighter's dancing yellow flame to what looked like an extra-thick gray bootlace dangling from the bottom of her charge.

Since she only had to get out of here and around the corner, fifteen seconds would be more than enough time. Otherwise she'd be out in the main passageway tapping her foot, listening to Cat wonder and worry and ask a thousand silly questions.

Well on the way to losing whatever passed for her mind, in other words.

The second the fuse sparked, Tansy turned to book it out of there.

And crashed solidly into Cat, still holding her damn boards.

# CHAPTER 6

BOTH OF THEM yelled as they crashed down hard enough to knock the wind out of Tansy's lungs and fill her mouth with the copper tang of her own blood.

"What the *hell*, Cat?" she shouted, blinking as Cat's headlamp blinded her, struggling to untangle herself from her own backpack. "I fucking *told* you to wait outside!"

"You were taking so long—" Cat wailed and twisted to the side, grabbing at her lower back. "Ahh *shit*, I landed on a damn rock and busted up my back!"

Tansy's internal countdown moved solidly into the red.

"I don't *give* a shit," she just about growled, finally scrambling to her feet. "Suck it up and come on, now!"

Cat made it onto her knees, and Tansy had to admit the sharp, fist-sized rock she'd landed on had to hurt like a mother.

"Just go *on* then, Tansy! I'll crawl out of here best I can. You said it wouldn't be all that big anyway."

Tansy tossed her backpack into the other chamber, wincing

at how many things she'd probably just jumbled into an unholy mess. For once in her life she was glad she hadn't taken the time to make a backup charge. And that one thing her Daddy had drilled into her mind enough that she still dreamed about it was keeping the safety on unless the blasted gun was in her hand and aimed at a target she intended to shoot.

"Doesn't have to be big enough to blow up a damn building." She squatted and grabbed Cat's scrawny arms and hauled her up, getting a shriek directly into her ear for her trouble. "You still don't want your empty damn head right underneath it. Now shut your mouth and *GO!*"

Tansy dragged Cat beside her, not giving a good god damn whether she kept her feet or fell and had to be dragged.

All the hairs on the back of her neck were stiff and prickling, and every nerve in her body was doing a tap dance on her brain.

They staggered through into the next chamber just as a sharp *POW* shoved her eardrums inward and drove a gritty breeze against her skin.

Tansy barely managed to skid herself to a halt before they crashed into the wall in front of them.

She knew she should be a lot more concerned at the way Cat scrabbled at that same wall and leaned over like she was ready to puke, backpack shifted over to one side and about to fall off.

Tansy probably *would* be concerned, once she got over being furious.

Or maybe when her damn ears finally stopped ringing.

"What the hell were you thinking, sneaking up on me like that? Who do you think could come and rescue us if we ended up with broken legs or worse? Exactly what do you think might happen if I decided to grab the steering wheel while you were flying around a curve like a dipshit bootlegger a hundred years too late?"

"I'm sorry as hell, Tansy." Cat's voice was way too loud, probably because her own ears sounded like a braying school bell that wouldn't stop. "I thought maybe something was wrong and you might need help."

A thick and shifting dirty-white cloud filled the air between them, turning Tansy's headlamp beam dimmer than driving through a thick fog at midnight. She had no idea whether she'd broken through into the museum's basement, but she'd definitely moved some rock.

She could barely see as Cat walked her hands up the wall and stood almost upright, lips drawn back and eyes squeezed closed. Tansy did her best to keep still and keep her mouth shut even though Cat seemed to have decided to freeze herself solid and stay down in the wretched coal-mine-turned-pot-mine forever. She finally moved enough to swing her backpack into place, then rubbed right above her non-existent backside with both hands.

"Gonna have a hell of a bruise there if nothing else," Cat said. "Did it work, Tansy? Are we still in business?"

Tansy snorted and shook her head. No one would ever say Cat Maybell didn't know how to keep her mind on her priorities no matter what else was going on.

She turned her headlamp toward the other chamber, where the dust was slowly starting to settle. Right now all she could see was a footstool-sized pile of muddy gray rocks on the floor beside the pale yellow of Cat's boards. She didn't hear any creaks or groans or anything else to make her think the whole roof was about to slip down.

No way to know until she walked right in there and took a good hard look.

She grabbed the steel bar with one hand and wiped grit off her face with the other.

They really should have had some kind of breathing masks for this job, but figuring out how to get a supply of them without drawing attention they didn't want cut that part of the plan short.

Tansy walked slowly into the other chamber, blinking to clear her eyes. She stepped over the biggest rocks so she wouldn't twist her own fool ankle and send the two of them hobbling out of here with not a thing to show for their trouble.

She poked at the ceiling a few times as she got closer to where she'd set the charge, jumping back when a couple of gravel-sized bits joined the pile on the ground.

Then her light moved past the jagged gray and reflected back a dull brown.

All the information she'd found on the museum and the house talked about work in the main part. How the foundation had been solid, the roof good despite how shaky it all looked from the outside.

She'd only found one mention of the basement. How it was nothing much more than a crawl space dug out during construction instead of a modern concrete room made to hold a furnace and water heater or a stupid man cave with a giant TV and bar and all kinds of other silliness.

Those steps down from the hallway she'd checked out

before were supposed to open out on access to the electrical system added on years after the place was built, and that was it.

Still, Tansy wasn't entirely sure about that until she jabbed the rod up and didn't feel it rebound in her hand like it would off of stone.

It gave and tried to stick this time, because it ran right into dirt.

"Hot damn, we're through the rock!" she yelled over her shoulder. "Just need to get the rest of the way up into the basement and we're almost there."

She knew Cat wasn't playing around about her back hurting, because she actually heard footsteps instead of nothing at all when Cat walked in.

"You brought that shovel, right?" Cat said. "The one that folds up?"

Tansy trotted back out into the passage and scrabbled in her now-filthy backpack, puffing out a relieved breath that nothing inside seemed to be broken. She dragged it back with her, then pulled out a foldable shovel and a cunning little collapsible pick-axe kind of thing she'd been carrying in her car for years now.

Just a little item she'd seen in a camping store down in Atlanta and thought might come in handy on some job or other a long time ago.

"Hang back and let me see if this dirt is loose. I made the charge a tiny bit stronger than I needed, so it should have done some of the work for us."

Tansy unfolded the pickaxe and took aim at the dirt overhead, hoping she wouldn't have to swing too many times. It was a hell of a sharp angle for her shoulders after lugging that backpack through the mine.

Thank the goddess of fuses and explosions, a thick chunk of dirt thudded down on top of the rocks. A few more hard swings and strong twists and pulls at the mucky brown brought a good bit more tumbling into the mine.

She stepped back to catch her breath, leaning on the pickaxe.

"Listen Cat, you still going to be able to take a boost up there with your back and all? Otherwise we can try to pile up enough of this mess to climb on so I can at least hook the ladder on solid."

One of the other special-edition tools Tansy had tucked into her pack was an old fire escape ladder her Daddy had modified when she was a kid. Now it had an extra-heavy-duty hook on one end with little spikes that would hold on to most anything. She'd used it for rock and dirt and wood, more or less for innocent purposes.

Cat turned from one side to the other with only a twist of her lips to show if anything hurt.

"I think I'll be okay if you're real careful."

Tansy nodded, then went back to prying dirt out of the museum's half-assed basement, hoping she wouldn't run into an unreported improvement like a stone or tile floor. Even linoleum or cheap carpet over plywood would be a pain in the neck she didn't want to deal with.

Their luck held out once again when she swung the pickaxe and jarred her shoulders when the tip made contact with not much of anything at all, sending the impact of handle against mud right down to her bones. A few more gouges with the pickaxe and the shovel cleared out a space big enough for the ladder and one of them at a time to squeeze themselves through.

"All right, get ready." Tansy shoved the pickaxe and shovel into her backpack, wiped her sweaty palms on her pants, and braced one foot on the pile of rock and dirt. "I'll boost you up, then hand you the end of the ladder."

To her credit, Cat made a clear effort to walk without hunching her back at all. She put both hands on Tansy's shoulders, carefully balanced one boot on the meaty part of Tansy's thigh, and pushed off with her other leg.

Tansy caught Cat's free foot with her hands and lifted, trying her best not to twist and hurt Cat's back even worse, or set her own to spasming. All while swearing under her breath at the sharp edge and cold muck of boots against her palms and leg.

A good hard *shove*, and Cat got her hands, then both arms up into the hole in the roof, grunting like a whole yard full of pigs ready for dinner. Tansy grabbed both feet now, barely managing to keep her chin out of kicking range.

"Quit swinging your legs! You just about knocked me down."

"I'm sorry." Cat's whisper was harsh and more than a little annoying. "Can't hardly get hold of the dirt floor."

"Then hold your ass *still* and I'll push."

Cat's headlamp strobed in and out of sight as she took to waggling her head around as if she had to move to make up for the terrible strain of holding her legs more or less still. But those more-or-less still legs let Tansy heave Cat the rest of the way up into the basement.

"What do you see up there?"

Nothing but shuffling noises, and more of those useless light strobes.

"Cat, come on. We can't take the whole night for this."

"Found the way upstairs. You want me to leave the lights off, right?"

Tansy closed her eyes for a few seconds and counted to ten, just like she'd seen her Daddy do so many times when people didn't live up to his high standards, strange as they might seem to anyone who didn't grow up with him.

Most of the time, in other words.

"Right. Someone might see, remember? That basement light switch might be hooked into something upstairs or even on the porch. We need to get in and out quick as we can. Ready to catch the ladder so I can get up there?"

More shuffling noises, and the light's beam stabbed down and right into Tansy's eyes again.

"Yeah, toss it up. I see a post I can hook it onto."

Tansy was surprised into keeping her mouth shut when Cat caught the hook-end on the first try instead of making her throw it a couple dozen more times. The ladder's chains and metal steps rattled through her hands before going slack.

"Got it," Cat said. "Reach me those boards, and you should be able to climb right on up so we can get on with it and get out of here."

# CHAPTER 7

TANSY PASSED the two pieces of pine and the rusty length of metal up to Cat, then shrugged into her heavy backpack. She grabbed the cool rungs of the ladder, hoping her arms would still be able to drag herself and the extra weight all the way up into the Country on the Clinch Music Museum and Gallery.

After a few pulls and slippery steps, Tansy's headlamp showed Cat peering up the short flight of rickety wooden stairs, not even pretending to pay attention in case someone might need a bit of assistance.

The rest of the basement was mostly empty, with only the hulking gray furnace in one corner and a gigantic white water heater in another. The walls were partly the same jagged stone as the house, partly more uniform cinderblock, with old wooden shelves shoved in here and there. No windows, but turning on any of the bare incandescent bulbs tucked against the broad beams and joists overhead still wasn't worth the risk.

From the chemical stink that overrode even the musty

aroma of earth, someone had been down here with pesticide or rat killer or something else sharp and foul smelling not too long ago.

The floor was the mostly smooth dirt Tansy expected, with a cloud of dust kicked up from her handiwork and Cat's running around.

It didn't occur to her until she was most of the way up, hands straining and legs trembling, that she should have been more worried about whether she and the pack would actually fit through.

And Cat still hadn't noticed Tansy jammed partway through the hole in the floor, hung up by her own backpack, arms and legs shaking so badly the ladder jingled underneath her.

"Cat. If you can drag yourself away from whatever it is you're doing, I'm gonna need some help here."

Cat jumped like a mouse scurried up her leg before she turned and hurried back the best she could.

"What's wrong, Tansy? Are you hurt?"

"Not yet I ain't. But if I slip off this damn ladder and fall back down into the mine I guess I might be. My backpack's hung, I can't move up or down."

Cat frowned and leaned forward, once again blinding Tansy with her headlamp. Tansy was too busy bracing herself to cover her eyes.

"I can't see where it's caught," Cat said. "Try moving to one side and I'll try to grab hold."

Hoping she didn't shift enough to slip right off the ladder after all, Tansy twisted and pushed to the right as far as she could, but the straps just cut harder into her shoulders. When she turned to the left, she felt something give way that thankfully wasn't inside her own back.

"Got it!" Cat yanked the backpack harder in the same direction, but didn't quite manage to dislodge Tansy's weak grip on the dirt and ladder altogether. Between the two of them, Tansy finally hauled herself up onto the cool dirt floor.

She slipped the blasted pack off and sat there panting, staring up at the collection of thick cobwebs decorating the wood above her. Cat hovered, but for a wonder she seemed to catch a clue that her usual questions and chatter wouldn't be a good idea right then.

"Doesn't look like anyone's too worried about this basement," Tansy said. "Might take them a day or two to discover they've got a new ventilation shaft all set up and ready to go. By then we should have a good lead on moving our treasures along to someone who'd be mighty damn glad to have them. And glad to hand over a fat paycheck for the privilege."

She finally staggered to her feet, barely managing not to either trip on the boards or step right back through the hole and end this whole expedition right quick. For a damn wonder, her crap-shack raincoat was hardly any the worse for its tight squeeze. Scuffed and muddy, and probably still as watertight as it ever had been.

"Thanks for helping me out of there, Cat. What's the door into the museum look like?"

Cat stood back with her hands on her hips, and Tansy decided not to tell her she had strings of dingy cobwebs looped into the perm-curls of her brown hair.

"Looks like a regular old wooden door to me. Opens in toward us like you said, so we won't be able to kick it open or anything like that. I got my usual tools for getting into places that might accidentally be locked up, but I'm hoping you remembered to bring a crowbar or something."

Tansy walked slowly toward the stairs, catching a couple of deep breaths at last despite the foul, poison taste in the cool air. The hinges on the inside of the door were rusty but solid, a contrast to the other side's shiny new doorknob she'd seen on her visit to the museum.

"The knob doesn't exactly sit solid," she said. "So they either didn't put it in right, or it was a cheap one to begin with. Probably both. No reason they should spend a whole lot of cash to lock a door that goes down to an empty basement no one can get into or out of."

Cat let out a snorting laugh before she smacked her hand over her mouth, but not for long.

"Got a whole new doorway in the floor down here now, don't they? Let me grab my stuff and see what I can't get done."

Tansy brought her backpack up the creaking stairs while Cat worked, just in case they did need the little crowbar she had tucked inside. She hated to have to actually break the lock and make it a lot more likely their activities would be discovered sooner than she wanted.

If they caught any kind of good luck to offset the bad they'd had so far, no one would figure out what had happened until a good long while after the museum opened in a few hours' time.

Cat saved her from all that worry by getting the door popped open with a truly disturbing display of skill and speed.

"There you go!" She turned and pumped her fist, eyes and

voice brimming with pride. "Guess they never saw Cat Maybell coming."

A whoosh of warmer, much fresher air full of pine-scented cleaner rather than harsh pest-killer spilled down the stairs toward them.

"Speaking of seeing," Tansy said, "just because neither one of us spotted more than a couple of security cameras doesn't mean they don't have something. So get out your ski mask, and we need to work quick, now."

Tansy hated to admit it, but she'd been hoping Cat would forget to pack the only item of clothing they'd disagreed about.

Much as she hated the itchy, stinking things she and Cat had dug out of her closet the night before, Tansy pulled a turd-brown one down over her face and neck. She was immediately convinced the damn thing was working to suffocate her with mothball stench, constrict around her throat, and drive her to squalling madness with wanting to scratch until her skin bled.

If Cat's shit-eating grin through the goofy mouth hole was any indication, she actually seemed to *like* the bright red version that surely mashed the cobwebs and her artificial curls flat against her scalp.

"Gloves too, right? So we don't leave fingerprints that Craigen and Vail County's finest law enforcement officers couldn't find even if you slapped them upside the head?"

Tansy nodded as they both pulled on blue latex gloves Cat had plucked out of a
kitchen cabinet stuffed full of an alarming variety of first aid supplies.

Tansy had been too unnerved to ask why there'd been so

many kinds of bandages, wraps, creams, and compresses, much less why there were several boxes full of gloves.

"Yep, but still don't touch anything we don't need to. Best not to talk unless we have to, and even then, keep your voice down. Headlamps too. Might not have much time once we get inside. We're after the Captain O'Quinn stuff, and that's it."

Cat rolled her eyes.

"You act like I wasn't in my own damn living room when we planned all this, Tansy. That or you think I'm too dumb to figure out whether to scratch my nose or my ass. You might want to remember this whole thing was *my* idea in the *first* damn place."

Tansy stared at her, with the thickest, queasiest doubts she'd felt since Cat brought the job up back by the river. When Tansy had let herself get caught up in a great big flood of excitement as fast and high as the Clinch River after heavy rain.

She'd known Cat pretty well when they were ignorant kids, but they hadn't spoken for years until she sneaked up on Tansy.

Was this whole thing a river full of fast-running bullshit she was about to drown in?

"Yeah, Cat, I remember. I also seem to recall you claiming to *need* someone like me to make it all happen. Otherwise you'd still be wandering around in circles trying to think up a way to get inside this place. Got it?"

Tansy wished more than anything that she hadn't mentioned the masks yet. From nothing more than eyes glaring back at her, she had no idea what was going on inside Cat's wily mind.

Meanwhile the clock was ticking on the remote security the museum might or might not have.

Cat frowned, then twitched her shoulders up in a part shrug, part shaking their spat off like water from a dog's back.

"Come on, let's get a move on. Otherwise we'll still be standing here posing and honking at each other like those mean old geese down by the river when the sun comes up and they stroll on in to open this dump for the tourists."

When Tansy didn't move, Cat sighed and patted her on the shoulder, hard.

"Yeah, I *got* it, Tansy. We're both in tit-deep on this little stunt already. That's why we're both here, and why we're splitting everything right straight down the middle. How 'bout we get going and make sure to not get caught?"

Tansy forced herself not to sigh right back.

And vowed all over again not to let Cat out of her sight.

"I guess the only other choice is to haul our sorry asses back through the pot mine and go home without a thing to show for our trouble. Won't get a second chance once someone finds the hole we put in the floor, either. Be sure to stomp your boots real good to make sure we don't leave a bunch of footprints, and let's go."

# CHAPTER 8

THE FIRST THING Tansy noticed was how much light streamed in through the museum's uncovered windows.

From the yellowish streetlights that didn't seem bright at all if she wasn't trying to sneak around where she wasn't wanted, and from the big hokey sign out front.

Even all the way at the back of the building, every speck of light seemed to reflect off every last surface inside.

The second was how quiet the whole house was, and exactly how squeaky and loud the wooden floors were as Cat trotted through the door and into the Captain O'Quinn room hot and heavy behind it. Maybe that was why they kept all that screely bluegrass and country turned up so loud, to cover all the noise of floorboards that would still be old no matter how hard they remodeled.

Her mind started right up with the whispers about how someone was going to just *happen* to be walking by at this downright unholy hour for a small town, and just *happen* to see their headlamps flashing around even though they were pointed down at the floor, and just *happen* to hear the shrieking floorboards all the way through the thick stone walls and pristine shiny new windows.

She jumped and almost made a good squall of her own when Cat bumped into her.

"Funny how I didn't spot a damn thing about your cantankerous cousin's Daddy back there at all. No pictures or nothing. You'd think he'd be all over the place since Vickie swears on her useless life that he was the only reason Captain O'Quinn ever hit it big as he did. Decide to grab something from up front after all?"

"Can't say I'm surprised they left that part of the story out. Nothing from up front. We don't want a bunch of pissed and rich Nashville types bringing their kind of heat down our necks. Our original plan's the way to go. But wait here, 'cause I *am* going to grab one thing right quick that might help us out."

She hurried up to the front of the house, covering her light with one hand to keep the beam extra low. She plucked one of the souvenir t-shirts—looked like a horrible shade of puke green—and tucked it under her arm.

Then she walked toward the converted kitchen, doing her damnedest to keep from jumping at every little creak and shadow.

By the time their headlamps reflected off the display cases full of Captain O'Quinn memorabilia (and junk), Tansy had her breathing about back down to normal, but an unpleasant clammy sweat coated her body.

At least the odds of someone seeing their lights had to be a lot lower with nothing behind the museum but an empty back yard and the trees behind it.

She dropped the backpack to get out her Daddy's old glass-cutting tools, which seemed like the best way to get into those cases without making a huge mess and possibly getting both of them sliced to bits in the process.

Until she'd seen Cat's skill with the basement lock.

"Think you can work the lock on these cases? I don't want to break the glass and get both of us cut to ribbons, but otherwise it's going to take me a few minutes to cut through. If you can do it, I can get started on the rest and we'll get out of here a lot faster."

Cat dashed away from staring at the gold record on the wall and hit her knees right beside Tansy.

"*Hell* of a lot faster is more like it." She tapped her stubby fingernail against a silver lock about the size of a nickel, with a silver bar out to the side. "Give me about ten seconds and we'll load all this crap up. Doubt it will fetch as much as that record, but I'd say our buyers will part with a little cash for it."

Tansy snorted at the idea of people handing over any kind of money for the stuff she probably would have tossed in the garbage if she'd come across it. But if someone was willing to throw a few bucks at them for a handful of shredded ticket stubs or beer-stained posters, she'd sure as shit take it.

She left Cat to work her questionable magic on the display cases and turned her attention to the real prize: the so-called gold record.

It didn't look nearly as impressive without the museum's special spotlight bringing out the mellow gleam, but Tansy didn't care. Some overeager collector with more dollars than sense could highlight it with a dime-store naked bulb or a high-voltage floodlight for all of her.

She'd done enough searching and snooping online last night to content herself that the market for Captain O'Quinn and the Confederates memorabilia was small but incredibly dedicated. And willing to spend enough money on the dumbest shit to convince her this haul would be worth all the trouble.

Not millions for sure. Should tip a good bit over the line into five figures, if they were lucky and Cat really had found buyers worth bothering with.

Enough to get her a ways on down the road, though, and not having to worry about finding a job wherever she fetched up next for a good long while.

But what she refused to let slip out of her mind in all the excitement of making it into the museum in the first place was that this particular frame was the thing most likely to have some kind of security attached to it.

Outside of the big-ticket items on loan from Nashville, of course.

Now wasn't the time to get the jitters enough to hesitate, but it wasn't the time to be a dumbass either.

She took the time to lean as close to the wall as she could get, looking for any kind of lights or sensors or wires.

Nothing she could see, which wasn't exactly a surprise in this little town, huge piles of grant money to build the museum or not.

Cat's happy giggle and the soft hiss of the glass display door rolling to the side meant that part of the operation was under control.

Time to take charge of the main event.

The record's wooden frame wouldn't move to either side, so it was probably secured by more than an ordinary hook. That was fine. She had tools that could cut through just about anything short of it being bolted to a steel plate that surely didn't exist in this formerly run-down house.

The wood was cool even through her gloves as she got her fingers situated around both corners.

The glass over the fake golden disc fogged as she breathed out through the mouth hole of the wretched mask.

Tansy pushed straight up, hoping that would do the trick without having to dig out any of her tools.

The frame stayed stubbornly put for a second, then lifted with a loud snap that made her heart thud to a stop in her chest.

No sirens or alarm bells or buzzers, and no blinding flood-lights or automatic doors or popup cameras.

But even before she lowered the frame and saw a weird black square about the size of a postage stamp with coppery and green squiggles inside, her hair stood on end all over her arms.

"I think we might have just run through the last of our good luck, Cat."

Tansy turned the frame with the sprayed-gold record inside upside down and carefully set it on top of the display case. Cat stood beside her in a flash, her fast breathing making it clear she took the warning seriously.

"What's that thing on the back there?" Cat said.

Right in the middle of the frame's top piece, between two

hooks that were indeed ordinary, sat the other part of whatever Tansy had just broken.

Disconnected was probably a lot more like it.

Same tiny circuit-looking square as the one still sitting on the wall.

Either way, she wasn't about to believe someone, somewhere wouldn't know the frame with the real treasure inside was *off* the wall now.

"I don't know exactly *what* it is, but it means we're about to cut our time short. Get what you think looks easiest to sell and let's go."

"Then get the hell out of my way so I can bust into the rest of these cases."

Tansy settled the frame on the floor instead and dug into her backpack. She had a hot and bright suspicion whatever she was looking at did more than hold the gold record on the wall. She'd be doing herself, Cat, and the potential new owners of this particular bit of Captain O'Quinn memorabilia a huge favor by getting rid of it.

"I got the napkins and the posters they scribbled all over," Cat said, her voice edging toward high and shrill. "What else can you fit in your pack?"

"Anything that's signed, or looks like lyrics." Tansy used a metal tool of her Daddy's that she thought might have once been a dentist's pick to pry at the edge of the plastic square. "Didn't I see one of those tambourines signed? One of the broken ones, maybe?"

She barely heard the jingly rattle as Cat grabbed at least one of the noisy instruments. The pick only dented the wood instead of lifting the device at all. She switched to a bigger flat-head screwdriver and pushed harder than she really wanted to.

The same internal countdown that warned her when a blast was about to go off was getting close to the red.

"I think I can carry this guitar." Cat pronounced it GIT-tar. "Long as you don't think it will make too much noise or block our way going out."

"One of the mandolins might be better. Smaller and lighter. Listen, can you try to get the middle out of this thing? I'm having trouble getting it loose, and I don't want to break the frame."

The guitar thumped to the floor with an out-of-tune *thrum*, and Cat leaned over the frame. Tansy sat back and wiped sweat away from her eyes with her sleeve.

"Can't we just prize it out when we get back to the car?" Cat said. "So we can haul ass out of here right now?"

"We could, but I think it might be some kind of tracker. Better not to take the chance if you can knock it loose real quick and leave it here somewhere."

Cat grunted as she pulled out a set of heavy pliers that looked like a giant rusty bird beak.

"If you ain't worried about saving it, I don't guess I have to be real delicate."

She squeezed the black box until the plastic shattered, then did the same on the other side, leaving only a few flat pieces around screws driven right into the wood. The rest of the tiny circuit board landed on the gold carpet.

"That should do it," Tansy said.

Before she could say another word, blue light reflected off the display cases.

Blue light from the front of the house, spinning in a lazy circle.

Dipshits should have come in without that as well as without sirens, but it was still time to bid this thieving party farewell.

Cat grabbed Tansy's arm.

"Shit, someone's out there."

"Yeah, that's not exactly a surprise, but I gotta admit I thought they'd take longer to get here. Grab your stuff and let's go. Don't worry about closing the cases, but lock that basement door behind us."

# CHAPTER 9

TANSY STUFFED some of the signed junk still on the floor into her backpack, parked it on her shoulders, and picked up the gold record. After a split second to think about it, she tossed the little circuit board thing behind one of the open cases on her way toward the open basement door.

Cat stood beside it, mandolin under one arm, bouncing on the balls of her feet and waving her hand in a blurry circle.

"Hurry *on* now, can't let them see which way we went."

Tansy took the time to drop the ugly tourist-bait t-shirt on the ground, then drag it back and forth with her foot as she went. It wasn't perfect, but at least the traces of dust they'd left behind got smeared around good enough to make it hard to tell which way they'd come and gone.

She flashed Cat a mock-salute on the way past, kicked the dirty shirt down the stairs, and heard the door click shut a second later.

"Got it locked," Cat said. "Wonder if those cops have a

key?" She yanked the goofy mask off as she walked past Tansy, sending her brown hair into even more of a fluffy mess. But the cobwebs stayed put.

Tansy dragged her own mask off, then pulled the sticky gloves off and stuffed them inside it. She scratched at her sweaty face and scalp, wondering if she'd ever looked forward to a shower more than right that minute.

"Won't matter here in a minute or so," she said. "Help me dig some dirt up before you crawl back down in that mine, won't take a second."

Tansy shoved both masks and all the gloves into her backpack, and pulled a roll of old canvas out along with the folded shovel and pickaxe. She took the time to slip her compact black handgun into her hip pocket, safety still on.

"Just scuff around the floor a little," she said. "I only need enough to put around the edges of this canvas. Won't hold up for long, or if they look too close. But someone who just shines a flashlight down here won't see it."

Tansy kept her mouth shut as Cat only dragged the shovel over the surface without doing much good at all. At least it might let her work off some of her nervous energy and settle her jumpy ass down. Tansy's own work with the pickaxe had enough dirt loose for her purposes in less than a minute.

"You go on down and I'll hand my pack down to you, and the gold record and the ladder." Tansy unrolled the canvas and picked up the old pine boards. "I think I can get down just fine without it."

Cat scrambled down through the jagged hole in the basement's dirt floor, but paused with her fuzzy head still in sight.

The squeaky old wooden floorboards made enough noise to

let them know more than one police officer had shown up to investigate. That had to be the local bunch from Craigen. Tansy doubted Vail County had any rent-a-cops to speak of, or much in the way of private security that would bother to show up so fast.

"They can't hear us down here if we don't get up to shouting," she whispered, waving both hands to try to catch Cat's attention. "But we're about to scrape the bottom of our luck."

Cat's eyes got wide, but for a damn miracle, she shagged her ass down the ladder instead of arguing. The faint clanky noise of the metal rungs couldn't be helped. They just had to hope it was far enough away from the cops to escape notice.

Tansy knelt and waited for Cat to take her backpack, then Tansy's heavier one, trying not to wince at the way Cat staggered under its weight. The gold record was next.

All she could do was hope Cat didn't notice her worry about it possibly getting dropped and shattered on the pile of rocks.

Cat disappeared with the wood-framed prize, and Tansy's gut clenched again with fear of getting double-crossed. Even though the idea of Cat Maybell making it all the way out of the pot mine and back to the car by herself was about as dumb as trying to turn an old coal mine into a giant greenhouse without anyone noticing.

Cat appeared again, empty-handed and waving her hands like she was trying to take flight. She almost managed to keep her voice to a whisper.

"Okay, I got everything out of the way. Hurry before they drag you away by your ear."

Tansy unhooked the ladder, taking as much care to be

quiet as she could manage. She had it rolled most of the way toward the hole when she realized her massive mistake.

Draping the canvas over the hole in the floor with the boards and metal pole underneath was going to be damn near impossible without something to stand on. And leaving the ladder attached and trailing into the hole in the dirt floor would be as good as a giant flashing neon sign declaring "The Dumbass Robbers Went This Way!"

Her stomach turned at having to admit it even to herself, but she'd spent way too much damn time worrying about getting in and getting the stuff, and nowhere near enough time thinking through how to get herself back out.

The door's loose knob rattling sent her just about jumping out of her skin, and within a hair of tumbling through the hole right on top of Cat. At least this whole crazy scheme would be over one way or the other.

Cat's hissing whisper almost made Tansy wish she'd fallen head-first and shut both of them up.

"Tansy? What the hell are you waiting for?"

All Tansy could think to do was shake her head and cover her mouth, never mind that all she wanted to do was smack Cat upside the head until she shut up. When Cat opened her mouth again, Tansy waved her arms and pointed toward the basement door.

Which still rattled in its frame.

Cat finally clapped both hands over her mouth.

Tansy threw the canvas over the hole, not giving a damn how much dirt found its way onto Cat's face when she scuffed her little pile across the canvas.

Then she picked up the ladder as carefully as she could and slowly backed toward the furnace in the corner.

The boards and metal pole couldn't be helped, but they didn't look all that different from the usual kinds of junk in an old basement. And odds were low the cops would have any idea what was *supposed* to be down here anyway.

Right now the only thing she could let kick around in her mind was surviving until the next minute.

And that meant getting her ass out of sight.

She crouched down and flipped her headlight off a hot second before the basement door finally opened and a much-brighter flashlight beam stabbed around the room.

But not before she spotted the blasted puke green t-shirt, standing out like a dusty vomit beacon where it had fallen under the stairs.

A woman's voice floated down before Tansy could move.

"...how else someone could have gotten in and out of here. You saw how all the doors and windows were locked same as I did. None of them tripped the alarm. That didn't happen until our robbers got all the way to the back room."

"Yeah, Deputy Salyers, I saw," a man answered in a patronizing, sing-song voice. "Now you tell me how your thief managed to zap himself into that dead end of a basement? While you do that, I'll be busy figuring out who all has keys and the code to the security system. Pretty sure we'll get all the answers we need once we get our hands on the security tape footage."

Heavy footsteps stomped overhead, and the bright beam slashed around some more, cutting through the dust that sifted down around Tansy.

All along the basement's cinderblock walls, outlining the heavy floor joists and tattered cobwebs. Pinning the dingy water heater and grime-caked furnace.

But not quite managing to pick out the filthy, ugly shirt lurking almost directly under the cop's feet. Or the oddly lumpy spot in the floor or the wood and metal that hadn't been there an hour ago.

If the woman with the big flashlight—Deputy Salyers—decided to flip the light switch and got a good look at the sloppy job Tansy did with the canvas or the torn-up dirt floor, or pointed the beam straight down, squeezing back through the hole wouldn't be a problem.

Tansy would walk right out through the front door, with a prize of brand-new silvery bracelets chaining her wrists together, and no more worries about making her rent next month.

# CHAPTER 10

THE MAN SHOUTED—SOMETHING about asses getting in gear —and Deputy Salyers paused for a second, then slammed the door hard enough to make Tansy's ears ring.

Not so loud that she couldn't hear stomping footsteps heading back toward the scene of their crime.

Tansy stayed right where she was for several breaths, not sure if she had even a trace of luck left. The good kind, anyway. This job seemed to round up enough of the bad that she was about to drown in it.

She finally reached up with a shaky hand and turned her headlight back on, blinking like a rat in the sudden light. She didn't realize her feet had gone all pins and needles until she tried to walk across the dirt floor and almost fell on her ass.

But waiting for the awful prickling to stop wasn't something she could even think about.

Dead-end basement or not, once someone got a look at the security camera footage and realized she and Cat hadn't used a window or a door after all, they'd be right back down those stairs.

No way they'd skip turning on the light a second time.

And the bright red countdown clock inside Tansy's mind let her know her time was about to run out.

She staggered away from the furnace, clutching the rolled-up ladder to her chest, hoping she wouldn't overshoot and end up crashing into the old pot mine.

None of the cops had walked back toward the back of the house, not unless they were a damn sight quieter this time around.

Tansy tried to kneel by the canvas but ended up hitting the dirt on her knees instead, almost managing to bite back a groan.

She barely heard Cat's whisper this time.

"Tansy? You still up there?"

"Still up here." She dragged the canvas away. "Think you can get ahold of this ladder? I'll fix things here best I can, then maybe boost you up to get it all into place."

Cat's pale face nodded and she held up her arms. Tansy ended up rolling onto her belly before she handed the ladder down.

She dragged the boards and metal pole next to the hole, and bunched up the canvas right beside them with dirt over one edge. No real way to get the dirt over the whole thing after all, but her best would just have to do.

A flicker of guilt drifted through her mind at the thought of someone coming down here to check to furnace someday and falling right through, but it was way too late to do anything about that now. Hell, maybe whoever found it would decide Creepy Old Man Vance dug out the hole himself, hoping to lure some poor kid inside and dispose of the body in the amazing new cave he'd discovered when he was done with it.

Nothing for it but to hustle herself and Cat away from here and do her best to keep them both walking around free women.

If they finally caught a damn break, they'd be out of the mine and back in Cat's run-down apartment before anyone checked the basement again.

Before that dangerous thought about good luck floated up and inspired the cops right back into the basement, Tansy grunted to her feet, then hunch-walked under the stairs. At this point, she wasn't sure whether to expect an enormous spider to land on her face, or to move too fast and knock herself out.

Probably both.

But she managed to grab the shirt with nothing more than a warning from her aching back about how badly it planned to seize up solid if she kept bending over like that after lugging a heavy backpack.

"I'm coming down," Tansy said as she threw the shirt through the hole. "Grab that damn shirt and get over to the side so I don't land on top of you."

"Hell of a time to go back for a souvenir, ain't it? Watch out for that pile of rocks so you don't tear your ankles up."

Tansy bit back her reply asking why the hell Cat hadn't been busy moving a bunch of those rocks out of the way to make one single thing about this whole fool business easier instead of harder.

A few seconds of peering down at the mess convinced her

she saw a clear enough landing spot. And if that didn't work out, then Miss Cat Maybell would have to help her hobble all the way back to the car.

She sat at the edge of the hole and scooted forward until her legs dangled most of the way, then rolled onto her belly again, thinking of how hard she'd had to push to get through with her backpack on. Without it, she should be able to keep a pretty good grip on the sides. About the only way she could think of to keep from breaking her ankles or worse was to let herself down easy as she could, as far as she could, before she let go.

"You out of the way, Cat? Way back, in case I go asshole over mouth hole?"

A weirdly manic giggle floated up out of the darkness.

"Far enough, I guess. Just try not to land on your thick head."

Tansy rolled her eyes but decided to keep her mouth shut.

She wriggled backward, digging her elbows into the dirt, then bracing herself against the sides of the hole she'd punched with her own specially made shaped charge back when all of this seemed simple and sounded fun.

Held her breath for a few heartbeats, shoulders shaking and cramping from the strain, daring to send a wish for help toward wherever her Daddy had fetched up once he left this world behind.

And Tansy let go and dropped into the abandoned mine.

For a longer stretch of time than she expected, she believed everything had gone just fine.

She was flat on her back, sure, staring toward what her headlight showed of the gray rocks overhead with one chunk missing. Back of her head aching, skull ringing like a gong from hitting the ground.

All that roof rock scattered around her, the biggest ones under her boots, and more jagged bits than she'd like under her thighs and backside. Hoping the bruises wouldn't have too many cuts and scrapes to go along with them.

Thanking whatever kind of god might watch out for the likes of her and Cat that her head hadn't smacked one of them instead of the gravely dirt.

But that all seemed okay.

Even Cat fluttering and squawking around her like some kind of pale, scrawny, redneck variety of a fuzzy-headed chicken didn't bother Tansy all that much.

"Quit fussing and let me get up, now," Tansy said. "I guess I'll figure if I'm okay or not once you let me move."

Once Cat finally settled herself down, Tansy went to turn onto her right side.

And that's when all the bad luck came calling at once, knotted up into a lightning bolt of agony across her back and shoulder.

"Aww *hell*, Cat," she whispered, or at least she hoped her voice was that low. "I think I tore something loose. That or I've got one mother of a cramp."

Cat fluttered back into sight, eyes wide and lips drawn back from her teeth.

"Did you land right directly on one of those rocks?"

"I don't think so." Tansy held as still as she possibly could. "Might have wrenched my shoulder on the way down, but didn't feel it 'til just now."

"Can you stand up? If I help you, maybe?"

Tansy shifted toward her left side, gasping at the pain.

"Try pushing from behind, help me sit up."

Too big of an area hurt to be a broken bone, at least she thought so. Despite all her years of questionable decisions, she hadn't ever cracked more than a couple of toes.

With more grunts and shoves and complaints than she would have put up with from anyone else, she finally stood not quite steady on her feet. The whole stretch of her right shoulder from her chest around to the middle of her back was a sheet of fire.

"How are we gonna get all this stuff out of here, Tansy? I don't think I can manage both backpacks, and the mandolin, and the gold record, too."

"Don't go chasing after a new problem before we solve the first one. You've still got to get up there and pull the canvas over that hole in the floor. It won't fool anyone for very long, but it should give us enough time to drag our sorry asses out of here. Neither one of us is moving fast enough to get away if they figure out where we went. Not until we get your lead foot back to your car."

Cat stared toward the basement, shaking her head the whole time.

"I can't get up that far. I barely made it before, remember? And now you messed up your back or shoulder or whatever it is. You can't hardly boost me up with one arm"

"I don't much want to, trust me. But that's what I got to do anyway. I think I can brace on one of those bigger rocks, maybe. We don't have much of a choice unless you want to try to sprint out of here with the cops blazing-hot on our trail. I don't remember you doing any better in gym class than I did."

"Well no, I never did take to running laps and all that bull-shit. I still don't see how you can boost me up without both of us cracking our skulls on the way back down."

Tansy went to drag in a breath to calm her jumpy temper, but ended up trying to twist away from pain like a knife stab-bing into her shoulder blade instead. That twist only shoved the knife in deeper.

"Okay then, sounds to me like you got all the ideas in the world about how to solve our mess of trouble. Go ahead and spill it so we can get a move on. Let's hear it."

# CHAPTER 11

CAT'S concerned frown collapsed into a scowl, and Tansy forced herself not to laugh at the way Cat shrugged and crossed her arms at the same time like an angry toddler. Mainly because if breathing hurt that much, laughing would knot her up in a gasping pile in the middle of all those rocks until the cops showed up to collect her.

"You don't have to be such a *bitch* about it, Tansy. It ain't like that's gonna help us no matter what happens. Go right ahead and boost me up, then. If it tears your shoulder the rest of the way loose, that's on you."

"Oh I know what all's on me, don't you worry about that. Now listen, all you need to do is un-bunch that canvas we brought to cover up the hole. I already got it where it needs to go. Just pull it over the opening and we're out of here. Unless you're really looking forward to a nice long stretch in a jail cell."

Cat stepped toward the pile of rocks and mud, but she shook her head the whole time.

"You swear you're not going to drop me? I already busted up my own back if you'll remember. Last thing I need is for you to drop me on my damn head."

It was pretty much every last thing Tansy could manage to keep herself from asking what possible difference that could make, when Cat's skull wasn't anything more than a solid hunk of bone. Probably in a voice loud enough for the cops to hear from all the way down inside the mine.

Instead she walked over to the rock pile with her right hand against her belly to keep her shoulder from moving any more than it had to. From the way the pain kept digging deeper into her shoulder blade, she suspected she'd strained something on the way down, and maybe set off a monster of a cramp in her unreliable back when she tried to get up.

"I'm not about to swear anything like that, and you wouldn't either. Not if you're being honest about it. It's not like I'm an expert at this part. I told you I'd get us into the museum, and I did that. Without dropping the whole house down on us, or all this rock either. Last time I boosted you up there, you tried your best to kick me right in the face, remember? So how about this. You help me pile up these rocks so I don't have to lift you quite so high, and make damn sure you don't swing your legs. And I'll do my level best not to drop you on your damn fool head."

Cat kept staring up at the hole in the roof, with little bits of dust floating through the white light of her headlamp. Her pale face was streaked with the same dust, and she still had gray cobwebs matted into her frizzy permed hair. Her narrow shoulders rose and fell before she turned to Tansy.

For a wonder, she'd finally figured out how to keep her headlamp aimed to the side instead of directly into Tansy's eyes.

"*Fine*, Tansy. I'll do the very best I can to not kick you in the teeth, no matter how much I might feel like it right now. Let's just get it over with before one of those pigs upstairs smartens up enough to figure out where we are."

She squatted with a grunt and started shoving the rocks together.

Tansy pushed at the biggest ones with her boot, eventually holding onto Cat's wiry shoulder for balance with one hand. She wasn't sure whether Cat's trustworthiness or her hopes to get herself away in her own surprisingly fast car instead of in the back of a police cruiser kept her from pushing Tansy off-balance on purpose.

When they finished, they had a more-or-less stable platform a good foot and a half above the mine's floor. Not great, but better than they'd started with.

"Okay, that's gonna help a lot." Tansy wiped sweat away from her eyes, probably smearing her face with more gunk. "Help me get that big flat one over there on top so I can brace my leg against it."

They managed to cuss and heave enough to lift the heavy chunk of stone into place, giving Tansy almost another foot of leverage.

She climbed up, once again balancing against Cat's shoulder. This time Cat was kind—or desperate—enough to hold onto Tansy's waist to help. Tansy settled her right foot on the highest rock, relieved to see how much they'd gained on that blasted hole.

"I have to use my left arm to steady you this time, but you don't have to reach near as high. Ready?"

Cat shrugged with a sullen set to her face that looked way too much like her old sourpuss asshole of a father. Turk Maybell had only kept out of jail because he was too mean to get anyone to help him cause trouble, and too sorry to get up to enough of it on his own.

Tansy couldn't stop wondering if Cat honestly thought she could get out of the mine by herself. This was a perfect opportunity to get Tansy out of the way with one well-placed kick, then scoot back to her crappy apartment. Even if she had to leave a bunch of the stolen junk behind, it might be worth it to her to keep the rest for herself.

The countdown clock inside Tansy's head blinking and setting off a muscle-knotting alarm wasn't doing a damn thing to help with her throbbing shoulder.

Cat finally grinned big enough to show how much of the dust and grit had made its way onto her teeth. Tansy took that grin to show how much of her usual hellraising spirit still kicked away inside her mind and heart.

"Well shit, it ain't like I started into this mess by myself, or could get out of it by myself even if I wanted to. I figure the best thing we can do is make sure we either *get* out, or go out fighting."

She stepped up onto their uneven platform, grabbed Tansy's left shoulder, and settled her boot onto Tansy's knee.

"Boost away, Tansy, and let's see what we can't get done."

"Don't take this the wrong way now, but about all I can do is grab hold of your backside to push."

Tansy let out her troublemaking-little-girl giggle.

"You go right on ahead. That'll be the most action my ass has seen in longer than I want to admit."

With a push against Cat's bony hind end, and biting her cheek against the wallop of agony from what now felt like the whole right side of her back, Tansy lifted until both of Cat's boots dug into her thigh.

She shifted her grip to Cat's skinny thigh, blinking away the dust that shifted down as Cat tugged at the canvas.

"I hear those footsteps again, Tansy. Someone's walking around up there, right over my head."

"Just get that canvas over the hole, that's all. Even if they decide to check out the basement again, it will take them a minute to find anything."

Cat's shifting and wriggling set Tansy's thigh to cramping almost as bad as her back, but she still didn't move.

"Okay, let me down," Cat said, wobbling so much Tansy's leg almost gave out. "I got it the best I could."

"Did you cover the whole thing?"

"Just put me down and take a look for yourself. We got to get out of here like you keep saying!"

Tansy let Cat grab her left hand and shoulder before she could quite manage to knock them both down. Once Cat had both feet on the ground instead of pummeling her thigh, Tansy stepped down off the flat rock and straightened out her throbbing leg before she aimed her headlamp up.

The canvas was wrinkled and twisted, and probably didn't look even a little bit like the basement floor. But she couldn't see anything past it. Couldn't hear anything, either, but that was hardly reason to relax this far down.

That would all have to do.

Cat was right about one thing.

They had to get themselves gone.

"Good job, Cat. Now get loaded up and we'll head out."

Tansy didn't like showing so much weakness, not one little bit, but she let Cat help with her backpack, swearing a ret-hot streak the whole time. She had to shift it around to the side to keep the sharp aching in her shoulder blade from taking her breath, and walking crooked was probably going to set her hips and knees to hurting too.

And again, it would have to be good enough.

Dumping the metal ladder and her Daddy's tools in one of the mine's side rooms would make the load a hell of a lot lighter, at least on her body, but she was determined to keep the tools at the very least.

She hoped she wouldn't have to change her mind before they got back out into the nighttime fresh air.

# CHAPTER 12

TANSY NODDED and pretended to be grateful when Cat offered to trade the mandolin for the gold record, the most valuable thing to come out of what was turning into a slow-motion trainwreck. Even if she couldn't wait to get the damn thing out of her sight forever, she didn't want it scratched or broken.

Cat listed to the side quite a bit herself even with her smaller backpack, but Tansy knew her overstrained back wasn't going to take much more.

Going through all this hell only to end up with a bunch of scrap wood and shattered glass might drive Tansy all the way crazy.

"I think I'm gonna have to sleep for a damn *week* once we get out of here," Cat said once they finally got back to the main part of the mine. "After I scrub my ass in a hot shower for a couple of hours."

"That sounds real good to me. But not until we get rid of all this stuff."

Cat glanced toward Tansy, not quite enough to blind her with the headlamp but close.

"Come on Tansy, I don't think I can manage much more than dragging myself home right now, and that's only if I can stagger out of this mine. No one around this little town will be awake for hours. No one's about to figure out the basement for a good stretch of time, and when they do, we'll be long gone. No need to get into a big rush right away. I'm about done in."

Tansy tried to shift the backpack off her left hip, then sucked in a breath through her teeth at the blast of pain in her shoulder.

"I know we can't go to the buyers you rounded up right now. I don't want to wait until much after the sun comes up either. We might have kept from leaving fingerprints or showing our faces on those cameras, or at least I sure hope we did. But the quicker we get rid of it all, the less chance of us slipping up and getting caught."

"You mean *me* slipping up, don't you?" Cat breathed out hard enough to make her lips flap like a horse. "I swear, no matter how many things I get right, you're gonna figure out a way to make it all wrong."

Tansy forced herself to stop counting all the ways this whole loony idea could still go wrong and kept walking.

"Did I say that, Cat? If that's what I was thinking, I'm sure you know I would have said it right out loud. The only thing I *did* say was we need to get rid of the stuff right quick. We're both worn out and beat up. I don't know about you, but I'm not going to be able to get any real rest until this is finished.

When people get that tired and it goes on for days, mistakes get made. How much better will you rest once all this crap is out of your apartment and the money's in your pocket?"

They'd passed a bunch of the mine's empty rooms and made it almost back to the heart of the secret pot growing operation. Almost out and gone.

But Cat's crazy idea wormed its way into Tansy's mind despite herself. They really could stash everything in a shadowy corner, get some real rest, and come back for it all later.

Still, Cat turning more stubborn and sullen than usual only made Tansy more impatient to get this job done and get away from Craigen.

Probably for good this time. As weird as this visit was going, she didn't want to chance the next one being even worse.

She couldn't imagine how, but Cat picked up on her thoughts so easily Tansy's head might have been made of glass.

"Yeah, and you'll just take your share and run, right?" Cat said. "Leave me here in case the local cops do a good job for a change and come after me."

Tansy shook her head, annoyed at having to do it carefully to keep her back from flaring up more.

"What did you expect? Did you really think I was going to decide to stay here forever? I say you should take your share and get the hell out of town. A fresh start always does me good. Might do the same for you."

Cat stopped, or more like she *tried* to and staggered a couple more steps before she got her forward motion under control. She put the wretched gold record down at her feet, carefully, then crossed her arms and glared at Tansy.

"What exactly are you trying to say right now? You wanting to run me out of the town I was born in? That I haven't left so I could run off all over the place for years at a time? You think you can dig up buyers and sell all this stuff on your own, do you?"

Tansy closed her eyes for a second as she stopped, trying not to stagger herself. She swore she wouldn't do it because it would show too much of what she was thinking, but she couldn't help looking the way they were headed.

The first room with the rotting remains of the grand underground marijuana empire was barely in range of her headlamp, and a drift of night air cut through the musty mine smell.

They were so damn close to getting out of here.

And Cat picked now to do her best to stir up some dumbass excuse for a fight?

"You're not making any sense, Cat. First you accuse me of wanting to leave, then of wanting to run you off. You got something else you need to tell me? Something so important that we can't finish staggering out of this damn hole in the mountain first?"

Cat drew back and got way too interested in staring down at the wooden record frame and her own feet.

"*Hell* no, not a thing I need to tell you. I just think it might be good of you to let me know what your plans are is all. You know all about mine."

Tansy ruffled her mucky, sweaty hair, not wanting to believe the suspicions picking up way too much steam in her mind. She put the mandolin down beside the gold record, afraid she'd squeeze too hard and break the neck on the damn thing.

That would be a real shame when it wasn't the neck she wanted to get her hands around.

"You got some reason you want to delay us inside this mine, Cat? Or maybe you only want to delay *me* in here. Got someone waiting out there who's not so much on my side? Already make arrangements with your buyers that you don't want me to know about, is that it?"

Cat lifted her head and stuck out her chin.

"My arrangements ain't none of your concern. I told you I'd take care of it and I will. Since you're getting all high and mighty and questioning what I already told you, that's all the information you're gonna get about it out of me."

"You don't *have* any buyers, do you?" The words barely made it out of Tansy's mouth before she realized it was the truth. "Haven't made arrangements with them, anyway, and might not be able to. You smooth-talked me into this without having any idea how to get either one of us out of it, or if we'd have a damn thing to show for it in the end."

Now Cat looked down again, and she actually kicked one muddy boot at the ground like a stubborn kid.

All while Tansy tried her hardest to keep from throwing up.

A whiney edge under Cat's voice sounded like a child trying to talk her way out of something even though she knew she was caught.

"I don't know that I would put it exactly like that. There's plenty of folks around here who'd give their right arm for a piece of anything Captain O'Quinn and the Confederates played or touched or even looked at. You know that as much as I do. They're all over those online auction sites and yard sales all the time looking for stuff, money falling out of their assholes they can't wait to spend."

"So your big plan is to put everything online, or set up a yard sale right here in Craigen? Or peddle your stolen goods as far off as Estonoa, maybe? Because I got a better idea, and a faster one, too." Tansy tried to hang on to her temper, but her voice got louder with every word. "How about we just knock on the door of the museum before it even opens today instead? That way we can catch the cops still investigating, right? I reckon they'll hand a reward right over and we won't have to go through all the trouble of finding a buyer at all!"

Cat cringed as if Tansy had taken a swing at her, which Tansy had to admit was crossing her mind in great detail. That would at least let off some of the anger and frustration.

Never mind that she'd end up in a groaning ball of pain on the floor if she tried to move either one of her arms that fast and hard.

"If you think back on it, Tansy, I never did exactly say I had buyers set up, did I? All I said was people would be real interested in anything we could get. Matter of fact, I seem to remember *you* saying it would be the easiest thing in the world to find them. But I guess you can't remember that part."

Tansy breathed in through her open mouth, then closed it with her lips pulled inside and over her teeth. It was everything she could do to keep from biting down hard on her own flesh and blood. A strange, bad old habit she thought she'd kicked years ago when she got sick of the inside and outside of her lips being raw and chewed to bits any time she got stressed out or nervous or upset.

"I didn't write it all down, Cat, and I can sure as hell see what a mistake that was now. I know you said something along the lines of it would all be taken care of in a day or two if I left it up to you. Silly me, I thought you meant the stuff would be *sold*. Never crossed my mind you meant we'd both be in jail so it wouldn't matter."

Cat's jutted-out chin started to quiver, leaving Tansy feeling like she'd be more likely to scream than puke.

"Well, what are you wanting to do, then?" Cat said. "Dump all this crap off right here under the ground and leave it? Fine, let's do that. I'll drive you back into town, putt-putting along under the damn speed limit like a grouchy-ass old man in a baseball cap driving a pickup truck. Then you can get in your own car and disappear. Won't nobody ever know you been *dumb* enough to spend time with the likes of me."

"I would *love* to do that if we could. Get myself gone and pretend I never got into this mess in the first damn place. Not because I'm dumb or even because you are, Cat. But because I got caught up in chasing the same old busted thrill that never did get me to anywhere good. Shorts out whatever kind of brain I've got and gets me into trouble every damn time."

Tansy stepped forward and gingerly picked up the gold record in its frame, now sporting an impressive layer of dust all over the wood and glass. Her back and shoulder hovered a hair below screaming pain as long as she held it mostly with her left arm.

"But we both made our choices," she said, "good and bad, and we're a big part of the way toward done. I'm only going to ask this one time, and I need you to think about it before you answer me. Okay?"

Cat stared at her with wide eyes, tears that might or might not be real making them too bright in the headlamps.

"Okay, Tansy."

"Is anything you told me about buyers the truth? Or are we going to have to scrabble around to find a way to move this stuff along?" Tansy held up one hand when Cat opened her mouth. "No, don't answer me or say anything else until we step outside this godforsaken mine. Like I said, take that time to think about it."

Cat's shoulders hunched forward, and she seemed to shrink, like she was aging backwards into that kid who got caught after all. She snatched up the mandolin hard enough to get a harsh twang out of it. But thank the gods of impatient people everywhere—or maybe it was just Tansy's dear old grouchy dad finally bothering to lend a hand—Cat didn't say a word.

# CHAPTER 13

TANSY SPENT the rest of the silent, painful walk trying her best not to flinch and jump at every shadow that moved under her headlamp's glare. Or to twist around at the weird echoes of their footsteps bouncing off the abandoned mine's walls.

Cat had entirely lost her ability to move without making a sound, each step a soft thud against the bumpy floor underfoot. The occasional jangle of the tambourine in her pack hit like a direct pluck at Tansy's already stretched-thin nerves.

They both slowed when the last bit of the tunnel gave way to the mostly empty space of the junky old metal shed with nothing but a few worthless garden supplies inside. The last separation between them and the outside world after what seemed like a lifetime spent under the ground and sneaking around in the Country on the Clinch Music Museum and Gallery.

And Tansy's last chance to at least try to do something

different if Cat really had sold her down the muddy Clinch River.

The dust stirred up when they'd come inside had settled out of the air, so her headlamp's beam shone more-or-less clear. Not a trace of footprints on the ground besides theirs, either.

None of that meant someone wasn't waiting outside, where it was still dark. But it wouldn't be for much longer.

"All right, Cat. I know I asked you to wait until we got all the way out. But I figure I need to know as much as I can before I show my face. Stick my neck out is more like it. Have a chance to figure out what you want to say to me, or anything else I need to know?"

Cat's eyes darted everywhere but at Tansy, and Tansy felt her heart speed up and her muscles try to tense and get ready for a fight. She'd have to do her best not to finally drop the big prize if she had to go for the gun, and her best wasn't worth much right at the moment.

Too bad what she'd pretty much be fighting would be to keep from landing flat on her face if she tried to run.

"I ain't got no buyers. Not yet." Cat stared toward the shed, still avoiding Tansy's eyes. "I did hear a lot of people talking about how much they'd love to get their hands on some of the stuff in the museum back when it opened. Some of them were the type to consider it nothing but good luck if something came their way, never mind if it might be a little bit less than legal. Less than legal would make it worth *more* to them, I'd say."

"The type to at least think about looking the other way when it comes to breaking the law, you mean. As long as they can get what they want. Like us."

Cat's gaze met Tansy's for a quick second, and she flashed an even quicker smile.

"Like us, yeah. That's the ones I plan to talk to. It's the god's honest truth that I wasn't trying to trick you, or double-cross you, Tansy. What happened is I had all this stuff in my mind for weeks, but I wasn't sure how I could manage to pull it off. Not 'til I heard you was coming to town, and I only figured it all out when I saw you that day beside the river. When we talked about it and got everything moving faster than I could get ready with buyers. That's all."

Tansy pursed her lips to keep them away from chewing range. She couldn't deny how excited Cat had been at every suggestion, how she seemed genuinely surprised with every new idea Tansy came up with.

Even with all Cat's quick ability to open locks and her huge amount of bendable morals, Tansy doubted very much she was that good of an actress.

And still...

Cat hadn't exactly been honest about what she'd figured out before Tansy showed up, either.

The warnings inside Tansy's head weren't nearly as red-alert as they had been when her shaped charge was about to go off, or when the cops were getting ready to open the basement door.

But a tingling uneasiness worked its way along her arms all the same.

Standing at the end of a tunnel leading to a hole blasted in the museum's floor with all the stolen junk wouldn't solve any of her problems, and it could make everything else a hell of a lot worse.

"Okay then, Cat. Here's another one to think about on the way back to your apartment. What are you going to do about getting the stuff sold? Assuming we make it back there before the cops see us with all this loot and we don't have to worry about it anymore."

Cat nodded too fast, twisting another uncomfortable thread through Tansy's middle.

"I'll think about that, sure thing. I guess we'll have to wait a little bit to let the heat die down, but we'll get it all worked out. *I* will, I mean, and you'll know every single thing the very second I do."

She smiled again and started toward the shed's door, still nodding and muttering to herself.

Tansy hesitated for a second, still aware she held the only thing out of their stash that the museum bothered to protect with an alarm, and probably some kind of tracker.

Depending on Cat to be honest *and* smart was exactly the kind of thing Virg Stidham would have shaken his head over as he frowned at Tansy. He'd had a way of saying something (or someone) was stupid that she'd never heard anywhere else.

She could hear him clear as a bell in her mind, saying "Well, that was *styu*pid," emphasis on the *styu*.

She hitched the gold record's frame higher under her good arm, raised her chin, and headed toward the door herself.

If her choices had indeed been *styu*pid, those choices were already made. All she could do now was face up to them and do her best to keep going.

Nothing for it but to drag out the ratty old flannel sheets they'd brought from Cat's apartment, and use them to cover everything up in the beat-to-shit-on-the-outside sedan's trunk.

Then do their level best to carry it all upstairs before the sun rose, or one or both of them seized up too solid to walk any more.

Tansy would give Cat a chance to get her buyers together, or at least to say who she thought they might be. There was still a weedy little chance of getting the stuff sold without finding more disasters along the way.

Walking out into the open air with all that nonsense on her mind was her next mistake.

# CHAPTER 14

NOT EVEN A HINT of dawn faded out the great stretch of stars in the dark sky overhead, and nothing broke the silence besides the rustle of a breeze shivering the trees around the abandoned mine.

Cat sat behind the wheel of her rust-bucket, big-engine sedan, gripping the steering wheel with both hands, staring straight ahead.

Tansy frowned at the tight, puckered expression on Cat's face, easy enough to see with her headlamp and the dashboard's faint glow.

At a whiff of menthol cigarette smoke in the chilly air, Tansy missed a step and almost stopped walking.

Neither she nor Cat smoked.

No engine noise or exhaust stink from Cat's car or anything else, but that didn't mean a damn thing. Wouldn't be all that hard to park far enough to walk in, and they'd been underground and in the museum way more than long enough for someone to do it.

Tansy forced herself to keep moving without a stagger, letting the gold record's frame slip down into her left hand.

Whoever it was hadn't jumped her inside the shed or as soon as she stepped out, which is what she would have done in the same situation.

Acting nervous was the best way to *get* nervous, and the best way to get herself and Cat hurt, killed, or worse.

So either there was only one other person out here meaning to cause them harm, or two who weren't exactly the best of planners. Not that Tansy felt like a planning champ at the moment herself.

"Best get the engine started, Cat," she called as she got close to the car. "That heap of yours takes long enough to warm up that we'll be out here until noon otherwise."

Cat shook her head a tiny bit, and her face crumpled like she was about to cry for real this time.

Tansy set the gold record down, leaning it against the dented front fender. As she bent, she gritted her teeth hard enough to make her jaw hurt worse than the spasm in her shoulder as she slipped her hand into her right hip pocket.

A faint crackle of gravels behind the car gave her more than enough warning, or at least she hoped it would be.

"Don't tell me you've got another damn flat tire." Tansy wished she had time to get rid of the backpack, but she didn't want to give whoever was back there another second to get ready. "Surely to goodness you've got a spare in the back, and not just the flat you didn't bother to get fixed last time."

She brushed her fingertips along the dusty side of the car as she walked, keeping the gun low against her hip. Now was the time for all those times going out plinking with her Daddy and practicing at shooting ranges wherever she lived to finally pay off.

Cat stared up at her through the smudgy driver's side window, eyes huge and lips drawn back from her teeth. One eye red and puffy, the right side of her mouth trickling blood.

Still shaking her head barely enough to see.

Tansy kept going, flipping the safety off with her thumb.

She hoped the twitching muscles all along her back wouldn't keep her from raising her arm fast enough if it came down to it. She'd never needed the gun in all the years since her Daddy had given it to her for her fifteenth birthday.

But she always kept it clean and ready just in case of a time exactly like this.

Again that crackle of gravels, moving away and around the other side of the car.

Tansy decided to take a huge chance and get rid of the backpack after all. If whoever was hiding wasn't brave enough to stand and face her, being able to move at least a little faster might make the difference.

She held the gun in her awkward left hand long enough to shrug the strap off her right shoulder, making sure her finger was far away from the trigger. She covered a grunt of pain with a cough.

Gun back in her useful hand, she lowered the pack to the ground beside the back tire, laying flat out instead of propped up. Someone trying to sneak a look under the car might miss it. But she didn't miss Cat's green pack and the mandolin already in the back seat with the drift of fast-food bags and other junk.

At the back of the car, the gravels under her headlamp were kicked and scattered, showing the darker layer underneath.

A scattering of cigarette butts explained the stink, and made her wonder just how smart the lurkers could possibly be.

Or how much they didn't give a shit whether she and Cat knew they were there.

The dust on the trunk and back bumper was mostly gone in a series of smudges, possibly from some kind of fight.

Tansy hoped Cat gave at least as good as she got.

She tapped on the trunk with her free hand.

"Want to pop the trunk, Cat? Doesn't look like you have a flat after all, but I want to get all this stuff stowed away so we can get the hell out of here. I've had just about enough fun for one night."

The driver's side window rolled down a couple of inches with a chattery squeal, and Cat's voice sounded more or less calm.

Hopefully she'd stay that way enough to keep from doing something *styu*pid, and give Tansy a chance to deal with whoever'd decided to sneak up on them.

"Aw hell, Tansy, you know this piece of shit's too old for something that fancy to still be working. Just bang it real good on the left side before you lift up."

Sure enough, a dent from repeated pounding on the car's dull finish marked the spot.

Tansy leaned as much of her weight to the right as she could manage without falling over or twisting her back any worse than it already was. She leveled the gun about where she guessed a person would be hunkered down.

A series of crunching footsteps moving around the front of the car let her know she needed to watch out on the other side.

She shifted that way and banged twice in the middle of the dent with her fist and dropped into as much of a crouch as she could manage, both hands around the gun's grip.

The trunk groaned its slow way up, but Tansy didn't bother looking inside.

Because the footsteps moved faster, and right toward her.

# CHAPTER 15

A LOW SHADOW darted past the driver's side door.

But before Tansy could step past the trunk, someone yelped and hit the ground.

Hard enough to skid face-down in the gravels at her feet.

Courtesy of her filthy, much-abused backpack.

Tansy stepped forward and braced one of her muddy boots on the person's back, right in the middle of a scruffy and faded denim jacket. Instead of the gun Tansy was so worried about, they only had a rusty tire iron big enough to be a survivor from the 1970s.

The ribs heaving for breath looked almost as scrawny as Cat's, and the spray of thin, dirty-blonde hair gave her a sickeningly good idea who it might be.

She had to be sure, though.

Before she could decide what to do about it.

"Exactly who the hell might you be? And what the hell are you doing out here?"

The not-exactly-clever criminal tried to squirm away from Tansy's boot, so she pushed down a little harder.

"Might want to answer me before I decide to stand on you with both feet. That or tell me which body part you want me to start with."

The squirming stopped, and a muffled, out-of-breath shout cut through the quiet night with pure poison.

"Pick a body part for what? Stomping on with your other foot while you already got me down?"

"Maybe. I might just do that, once I'm out of bullets."

The pale white hand gripped the tire iron tighter for a second, trying to drag it across the gravels. Probably in an attempt to swing it at Tansy's other leg.

She twisted her boot against the denim jacket and the spine and ribs underneath, enough to make her point.

"Drop it. Or I'll start right now with your hand."

A furious grunt, and the tire iron landed a couple of inches away from the hand.

"All right. All *right*. Just move and let me catch my damn breath before you break my back!"

Tansy stayed where she was for a few seconds, certain she knew who she was dealing with from that voice. Then she stepped back, bringing the gun back up where it was clearly visible.

The person on the ground dragged in a few breaths, probably getting a mouthful of mucky dust, then pushed up on both hands. Then sat back and brushed the stringy hair back.

Tansy had never been more disappointed to be right in her entire life.

Her mean-as-hell, nothing-but-trouble cousin Vickie glared up at her with red, puffy eyes.

"Can't say I'm surprised to see *who* you are," Tansy said. "Now how about you get busy telling me what you're doing out here. Besides causing trouble, which is even less of a surprise."

Vickie leaned to the side and spat dust.

"What the hell do *you* care, Tansy Marie? This is a public place, right?" She put both hands to her cheeks and widened her eyes. "Wait a minute, it's actually not public at all, is it? Last time anyone got use out of it was for a crime scene. So it's pretty damn rich of *you* to ask *me* what I'm doing here. You don't even live in Virginia anymore, ain't that right?"

The car shifted on creaky shocks, and Cat got out.

"*I'll* tell you what she was doing. She was hiding behind my car like some kind of skunk, or maybe a possum that's got a good load of rabies on board. Too stubborn or dumb to leave off smoking her nasty cigarettes, or I never would have known anyone was there. Jumped me before I could say a word or get away."

"That does sound awfully rude to me," Tansy said. "Especially for someone who I'm going to guess is out on work release or probation or something like it. Be a real shame for your probation officer to find out about you skulking around out here this time of night. Even if you didn't do the best job of keeping yourself hidden. I sniffed out your menthol reek before I got anywhere near the car."

Vickie started to push up off her knees, but stopped when Tansy raised the gun a little bit higher.

"Suppose *you* got a great reason for being out here in the

middle of the damn night, Tansy? With this lowlife that don't have the sense to scratch the damn cobwebs out of her Q-Tip hair?"

Cat brushed at her hair, missing most of the matted-flat cobwebs, then stood beside Tansy.

"What the hell does it matter why me and Tansy are out here, Vickie? We didn't sneak around behind a car and jump you!"

Tansy nodded. "She's got a point. Might want to get to talking before the cops find their way here."

Cat managed to keep from looking surprised, but Vickie scowled.

"What makes you think I was *trying* to sneak? No need for that with you two dipshits. I didn't hardly care if you knew I was here or not, and it sure don't matter now. I don't see why any cops would be out here this time of night. Unless your cowardly ass called them."

"They might just happen to be out here on other business," Tansy said. "And it sure does look strange, you running around in the middle of the night when surely you want to be on time for your work-release job tomorrow."

Vickie sat back on her heels and crossed her arms. And Tansy wondered if her dumbass cousin showing up might give her and Cat a way out without leaving a trail behind them.

"You're just about mean enough to turn me in no matter what I do," Vickie said. "So you and your little friend here can have a good laugh about it. But I bet the cops would be real interested to hear about what all you bought down at the farm supply the other day."

This time Cat did stare at Tansy, eyes and mouth tight with fear.

"Nothing a whole bunch of people aren't buying every day, Vickie," Tansy said. "Gonna have to do better than that."

"I guess I'm doing pretty damn good going by the way Cat's shitting her pants right about now. See, the trouble is a whole lot of folks knew all about your Daddy's little habit of blowing stuff up, Tansy. Uncle Virge never bothered to teach me or anyone else all the things he taught you about making things go boom, but I don't have to be some kind of genius to know what you was shopping for."

"Got some way to prove that?" Tansy said. "About me or my Daddy? Because otherwise I'm pretty much done wasting time with the likes of you. Gotta get back and make a call to that parole officer."

Vickie shifted from her heels to sitting on one hip, still scowling up at Tansy. But she soon enough turned her spiteful focus to Cat.

"What, you two out here trying to pick up where Cat's dumbass Uncle Casey left off? Think you're smart enough to set up the damn pot mine all over again?" She let out a harsh laugh that echoed back from the old shed. "I sure as hell doubt you two could manage much more than getting yourself killed under the ground."

Cat stepped forward, fists clenched.

"Whatever my uncle or anyone else in my family did ain't none of your damn business!"

Tansy touched Cat's arm and shook her head.

"Not a trace of pot or anything else on us," she said. "You and the cops and anyone else can go right ahead and search.

What I want to know is what you thought you were going to get out of following us out here. I don't believe for one second you just happened to be in the neighborhood in the middle of the night."

Vickie shook her head and chuckled, then brushed her dusty hands off against her jeans.

"What, so you can tell my idiot parole officer all about it? That's the thing about you, Tansy. It's not just that you always think you're the smartest person around. It's how you have to decide everyone else is a dumbass so you can believe that. Thing is that big old brain of yours messed up by coming by my *work-release* job as you so kindly put it. Messed up even more breaking into that museum. Don't think I didn't get a look at what Cat was hauling."

Tansy kept herself from so much as glancing at the gold record Vickie had raced past, but that didn't much matter. No one was likely to believe Cat would randomly be carrying a professional-quality mandolin around at any time, much less on an abandoned road in the middle of the night.

Best to keep Vickie off-balance and edging toward angry, when her thinking was sure to turn into nothing but cunning and fire.

"So you followed us out here, huh?" Tansy said. "Trying to lend the fine folks in local law enforcement a hand for a change instead of running them ragged trying to keep up with your latest crime spree? That's about as believable as you stirring up bullshit for *years* claiming Mamaw and Papaw's neighbors decided to buy that rotten Harbury place out from under you. One you never have even *tried* to buy yourself all these many years later."

"You go straight on to hell, Tansy. You don't know a damn thing about any of that. 'Course you'd take anyone else's side over mine no matter what the truth was."

Vickie kept laughing, but she clenched her fists against her legs.

Cat seemed to pick up on the theme, or else she'd already used up her short supply of calm and logical thought.

"Or maybe you figured you could get in on the action and get your hands on some of the junk from your Daddy's band. They got a *real* nice display at that museum, but I never did see a thing about him writing their music or tuning their guitars or cleaning their toilets or whatever the hell you seem to think he did."

The laugh died in Vickie's throat, and her eyes narrowed.

"Now didn't you just say leave family out of it, Cat? And there you go running your mouth about mine. The good ones, I mean, not this worthless bitch you took such a liking to all of a sudden." She looked at Tansy, eyebrows raised. "If you think you might could see your way clear to allow it, I'd like to get up off this nasty ground now."

She pushed against her thighs and raised up, starting again with that irritating chuckle.

Tansy shifted her feet to get balanced and opened her mouth to warn Cat.

But before a word made it out, Vickie lowered her head, sprang out of her crouch, and charged toward Tansy.

# CHAPTER 16

THE COLLISION KNOCKED Tansy off balance and the rip of hurt in her back kept her that way.

Sending both of them crashing down over her own blasted backpack.

Vickie turned into a twisting mess of knees and elbows, and what felt like at least ten hands scrabbling and clawing to get Tansy's gun.

Cat screamed out a warning.

And the gun went off between Tansy's body and Vickie's.

Tansy couldn't hear a thing through another bout of harsh ringing in her ears.

The pungent stink of gunpowder burned her nose.

Huge, jagged gravels laid down years ago to support coal trucks dug into her head, back, and legs.

And for one awful second, she wasn't sure where the bullet ended up.

Because a sharp agony burned across her left side just

under her ribs, even worse than the massive screaming knot in her right shoulder.

All her mind could make sense of was what Cat had shouted right before the gun cut the brawl between Tansy and Vickie short.

*"Knife!"*

Then the weight on top of her heaved, and Vickie let out a strangled cough.

Tansy struggled and pushed until Vickie finally toppled away and onto the gravels.

She still couldn't hear a thing, but she saw Cat's mouth moving as she darted forward.

The word looked like *knife*, over and over again.

Cat danced back, and she did have a bloody blade about eight inches long in her hand.

Tansy managed to loosen her painfully tight grip on the gun enough to drop it. She reached toward the pain in her side, and her fingers came away red in the light of her headlamp, shoved sideways in the fight.

Her whole chest and belly were sopping wet with blood.

Nausea and dizziness rolled through her.

"Mine?" she said, her voice not much more than a rumble in her throat. "Is all that blood *mine*?"

Cat squatted beside her, shaking her head.

She pointed at Vickie.

Just as Vickie coughed out a great crimson bubble.

Tansy's gut threatened to reverse gears on everything she'd eaten over the last day. She was hardly a medical expert, but she knew blood coming out someone's mouth wasn't a good thing.

Cat pointed at the car, and her mouth kept making the

shape of the word *go*. Over and over again. Her throat swelled enough that Tansy knew she had to be shouting.

Tansy assumed she groaned from the rumble in her chest when she tried to get to her feet, and from the way Cat finally dropped the knife, stopped her fussing, and squatted to help.

"We need to get out of here, I know," Tansy said as she staggered over to lean against Cat's car. "Just give me a minute to catch my breath. And think about what we need to do."

Cat rolled her eyes, and Tansy barely heard the words this time.

"We got to *go*, Tansy! Right *now!*"

Tansy lifted the cheap rain jacket and her shirt, hoping the long, neat slice in the fabric of both didn't show up quite as nasty on her flesh.

Not quite as bad, anyway, but she did have a vicious slash as long as her hand in the soft part between her ribs and hip.

All of her insides were still where they were supposed to be, but damn if that didn't burn like a bitch.

"Good thing Vickie's aim wasn't that great. With the knife at least. Looks like she did a whole lot better with my gun."

Cat scowled, but only for a second. She tried to fight it, lips and chin trembling, and she even covered her mouth.

But a wicked smile finally won out, and her words made it through the ringing this time.

Turned out having a gunshot muffled between two bodies kept it from deadening her ears for more than a minute or two.

"That's *awful*, Tansy. I think she might be dead."

Tansy glanced over long enough to verify her cousin's gory chest wasn't moving. Which was a good match for the way her eyes stared unfocused at the dark sky overhead.

She wasn't surprised to see Vickie's face scowling and bitter and angry, like it had been since they were kids. From her own memories and tales her family told, Vickie had tussled and scrapped and backstabbed and taken every chance to cause trouble pretty much since the day she squalled her way into the world.

No doubt she would have been pleased as pie to properly stab Tansy if that bullet hadn't put an end to her roiling anger at long last.

"I'd say you're right about that. Honestly, I'm not one-hundred-percent sure which one of us pulled the trigger. If it was me, I didn't do it on purpose. And I doubt hardly anyone would kick up a fuss if either one of us just disappeared. Except maybe her last parole officer in a long string of them. But we really can't leave her sprawled out on the ground like that."

Tansy didn't realize how much the shakes had set in until she tried to press her shirt against the blood still welling out of her side. The tremor felt like it was going to settle into a good case of teeth-chattering and shivering before too long.

Yeah, she'd always known her interest in blowing things up and taking things down could potentially result in a body count. As far as she knew, it never had.

And even *if* it had, lighting a fuse or setting a timer or clicking a detonator was nothing at all like having a person bleed out all over her.

Getting too caught up in the horror of that—never mind questions of who might deserve their fate or not—wasn't going to help her or Cat get out of this waking nightmare that now featured a corpse without their hands held nice and secure behind their backs.

"You want to haul her off somewhere?" Cat didn't seem anywhere near as shook up as Tansy was starting to feel. Not that anyone who knew her would be surprised by that. "I know my car's a piece of shit, but I wasn't exactly planning to soak it down with blood and guts."

"I don't guess we have to do all of that, not with an abandoned coal mine right here in front of us. We could just drag her in there, don't you think?"

Cat put her hands on her hips and stared toward the old shed.

"What if that draws the cops inside, and right to the hole we blasted in the roof?"

Tansy shrugged. Plenty of time for reflections on blame and sin and mortality later.

Preferably alone, and with something stronger than beer to keep her company.

"What if it does?" she said. "With a record like Vickie's, it wouldn't be too big of a leap to decide *she* was the one who broke in. Everyone in town and the whole county and probably all the way into Kentucky and West Virginia has heard her carrying on about her Daddy being the genius behind the whole Captain O'Quinn thing."

The cold logic of it unnerved even her, even though she'd been wondering how to pin this whole thing on Vickie only a few minutes ago.

"Even with what they saw on the security camera," Tansy went on, "her build and hair are close enough to mine to pass. Hell, they might even decide she got into a fight with whoever helped her out. They killed her, then took off with the prize."

Cat tilted her head to the side.

"I reckon as long as we're real careful and wear gloves, that might work. We could even put one of those ski masks on over her head to make it look better." She flashed her wicked smile and let loose with the now-eerie little-girl giggle. "Think the cops or museum or someone else might send a reward our way if we tip them off to where she is?"

Tansy couldn't stop her face from twisting into a frown at the thought of going *that* far to take advantage of what happened, at least right then. Not enough of one to argue with Cat about it, though.

"You never know, Cat. They just might at that. Whatever we work out, I got to get out of these bloody clothes. The smell is making me want to puke."

Cat wrinkled her nose, then winced. She gingerly touched it, followed by her eye and her lip.

"Your mean-ass cousin did a number on my face, I can tell you that for sure. Probably should get her moved before you change. I guess we could leave that jacket in the mine."

Tansy shook her head as she slowly walked toward Vickie.

Or what used to be Vickie.

"I don't want to leave these clothes anywhere the cops might find them. It's mostly her blood, but she sliced me pretty good. On the off chance a local cop knows what they're doing and checks for DNA, I might just get busted. Maybe for murder on top of the damn robbery."

"Nah, self-defense. No way anyone would call it murder, not with her record." Cat stood beside Tansy, both of them staring down at Vickie. "I never did know her people very well. Were they as ornery as she was?"

"Not really. Uncle Arn could be short-tempered, like my

Daddy, and Aunt Syl was downright snappish before she had a big cup of her high-test coffee in the morning. But I never saw or heard of them being worse than anyone else's parents around here. No one ever could figure out what went so sour with Vickie. Here, let's get her feet. Supposed to rain today, so I guess the blood will get mostly washed off these gravels. I hope so, anyway."

# CHAPTER 17

CAT PULLED out four more blue latex gloves from her endless supply, and Tansy was glad to put them on this time. Even with her hands already coated with muck and drying blood, she didn't want to touch anyone's dead body if she could possibly avoid it.

They both squatted—Tansy slowly and carefully to keep from setting her back off worse than it already was—and each grabbed hold of one foot.

Tansy couldn't help noticing Vickie wore grubby white sneakers with bright yellow socks underneath for some reason. Kind of a sad choice for a laying-out wardrobe. Even if the laying out would be in a hole in the ground no one else remembered anymore.

Not that Vickie had plans to be the one drawing her last when she set out for whatever she'd planned to do once she caught up with Tansy.

"We'll have to look out for her car, too," Cat said. "I doubt she walked all the way out here. Or does she even have a license these days?"

Tansy grunted as they got Vickie moving with a good tug. Hardly any blood was on the gravels after all, probably because most of it what wasn't on Vickie's chest was all over Tansy.

"No idea about the car or the driving. Might be a good thing if she did leave something on the road out here, though. I kinda doubt either one of us is up for any kind of reward, but it might make sense to tip off the cops once we get back to your place."

Tansy focused on Cat so she didn't have to pay attention to the way Vickie's hair slithered over the gravels, or the way her head bobbed and jounced as they dragged her along.

"We *can't* call from my phone, Tansy. You know they got ways to trace things like that. Maybe one of those burner phones I keep seeing at the discount store in town."

"Sure, a burner phone is fine. Probably grab a couple of them so you can get in touch with all those buyers."

When Cat glanced over, her face tight and fearful, Tansy winked and managed to smile.

"Well yeah," Cat finally said. "That would make a whole lot of sense. Might talk to some of them face-to-face, but only the ones I know won't turn bad on us."

The going got a lot easier inside the shed and off the huge gravels, and they got Vickie inside the mine without too much trouble. Tansy liked the idea of taking her all the way under the museum's basement, but her back and legs and even her nerves had different ideas.

By the time they gave up beside the rotting bits of the pot mine, she trembled from head to toe for a brand-new reason than the shock and disgust of having her cousin pretty much die on her chest.

"That's going to have to do it, Cat. I'm a little bit past running on empty already. Just walking back out to the car is gonna do me in."

Cat must have been running out of gas herself, because she didn't argue or even comment. She just nodded.

"Reckon we should turn her over on her belly at least. I saw on some cop show or other how the blood pools inside, and that's how they can tell a body's been moved. Won't be near enough blood in the dirt, but we can't much help that. Maybe look in her pockets for the car keys?"

The things Cat thought of and what she was good at continued to give Tansy chilly surprises, almost as much as what she was willing to do herself.

But she was more than happy to let Cat squat down to handle the morbid search.

"Yep, keys right here," Cat said when she reached into Vickie's hip pocket. "Or one key, I guess I should say. Looks like your cousin had a Ford new enough to have a fancy push-button starter. Can't tell from this if it's fast enough to be worth taking with us instead of my old heap that I know so well."

Tansy took the rounded rectangle of black plastic with the blue Ford logo on one side. It looked brand new, without a single scuff or scratch. Several regular metal keys jangled on the ring, but they looked like ordinary house or office keys.

Unless she'd changed mightily since the last time Tansy spent time with her, Vickie kept her cars in a lot worse shape than Cat did, outside and under the hood.

"Assuming this is actually *her* car," Tansy said. "And not one she just happened to 'find' unoccupied, and borrowed for this little expedition." She pulled out a long, chunky brass key and held it up. "Unless I miss my guess, this one goes to a safety deposit box or something like it. I never knew Vickie to bother with anything like that."

"You might be right about that." Cat held up a tattered wallet made out of cheap, scratchy brown fabric. "Nothing but a state ID in there. No driver's license. Probably find a lot more in this other one."

This time she held up a black leather oversized wallet—the kind women sometimes carried with a little calendar inside— that was far from cheap or tattered.

Tansy's stomach gave another tremendous lurch, and she shook her head.

All at once she had no desire to even touch the wallet, much less flip it open and find out who it belonged to. Probably the same person who would surely be wondering where their Ford was before too much more time passed.

Cat shrugged and dropped the wallet on the bumpy floor of the mine tunnel.

And the countdown in Tansy's head started up again.

"I think we should put those back and get out of here, Cat. Forget about putting one of those masks on her or anything else. Seemed like a good idea to check her pockets, I know. But even the local cops around here will find that hole in the museum basement before too much time goes by."

"Yeah, that one woman cop had it figured out right off the bat, didn't she? Long as Vickie didn't park whatever she was driving sideways across the road to block us, we ought to be able to get out just fine."

Tansy tried to keep her feet still, but the urge to head back toward the mine entrance was getting to her quick. It was all she could do to keep from grabbing Cat and dragging her backward before both wallets and the keys were stuffed back in Vickie's pockets.

She didn't hide her agitation nearly as well as she thought.

Cat finally got to her feet, brushing her gloved hands against her jacket.

"You hear something, Tansy? Or see something? You're jumpy as hell even standing still for some reason."

"Not hearing or seeing anything yet. But I don't like hanging around here right between the robbery we committed and the murder anyone who finds us will probably decide I did from the looks of me. Time to get out of here and lay low for a little while, I think."

Cat walked past Tansy, shaking her head and talking under her breath.

"Already *told* you to call it self-defense..."

Tansy started to follow, then stopped, turning her whole body enough to aim her face back toward the museum.

Nothing except her own heartbeat and Cat's footsteps.

She couldn't smell a thing besides sour sweat and the awful, metallic stink of blood she'd much rather not think about.

Then a red alert wound itself up inside her head.

She wasn't making any noise, either, not standing there.

But she *was* pointing a bright white headlamp into a mine

that had been empty for years, straight back toward the hole she'd punched in the museum's basement.

Not exactly the best strategy when it came to keeping herself hidden.

She took a deep breath and clicked her headlamp off, keeping her eyes pointed down the tunnel as long as she dared.

Her ears warned her before her vision adjusted.

Instead of the silence of a long-dead coal mine, she caught the faint echo of something moving.

And the distant rise and fall of voices that let her know she wasn't hearing some kind of racoon or bear or skunk that somehow managed to sneak in behind her and Cat.

Her heart thudded its way into her throat, blocking her chance to hear anything else.

Not that she needed any more reasons to get her ass in gear and away from the scene of one too many crimes.

She looked down and switched her headlamp to dim, and immediately covered her mouth to stop a squeal from letting everyone else in the mine know exactly where she was.

Tansy had come within a hair of tripping over her cousin's body and sprawling face-first on the muddy ground right beside her.

She got herself moving, holding her arm tight against her side to keep her shoulder from wrenching a groan out of her.

Because no matter how it or the slice on her other side hurt, she had to get a damn move on. Not only because she had no idea how fast the cops might be coming up behind her, or whether they'd already called in another car or several to check out the open end of the mine.

All her nerves and muscles and mind and everything else

were tensed up with the certainty that Cat was going to yell back after her, or honk the horn, or something equally impatient and thoughtless. Might as well call it dumb at this point.

And more than enough to bring all the hellfire they deserved and more raining down on their heads.

## CHAPTER 18

TANSY WAS HUFFING and puffing more than she wanted to admit by the time she made it out to the old shed not a second too soon.

Cat was indeed standing in the doorway, hands on her hips. Tansy would have bet every penny of whatever they might finally manage to sell all the Captain O'Quinn junk for that Cat was about five seconds away from that disastrous shout.

"*There* you are," Cat said, slumping against the side of the doorway. "I was about to call for help, only I couldn't think who I ought to call."

"No time to call anyone, unless it's the one call from a jail cell. Couldn't prove who it was, but someone's coming along behind me. One guess who."

Now it was Cat's turn to smack her hand over her own mouth. She waved Tansy on with her free hand.

"Moving as fast as I can. Think you might go get the car started, Cat?"

With a fierce nod that had to make her head hurt, Cat turned and scurried outside.

Tansy hadn't realized how worried she was that the junker really wouldn't start until she smelled oily exhaust and saw cockeyed headlights.

When she half-hobbled outside, Tansy laughed so hard she let out a yelp of pain after all.

For once, Cat Maybell had done exactly what needed to be done even though Tansy hadn't asked her or reminded her.

Neither the framed gold record nor the backpack were still outside the car. Cat had even remembered to grab Tansy's gun from where she'd dropped it on the gravels.

She paused long enough to strip off the disgusting rain jacket, still giggling, and turned it inside out to contain the mess the best she could. Then she let loose with a proper guffaw when she noticed the bargain-basement fabric had stopped the blood from getting through to her shirt every-where except where Vickie's knife did the job from the inside out.

Cat stared hard when Tansy pretty much fell into the passenger seat.

"What the hell's so funny? Don't you *tell* me we forgot something in there."

Tansy shook her head.

"Nothing like that. I have to take back everything I said about these cheap crap-shack raincoats is all. Appreciate you getting the rest of the stuff loaded up on your own."

Cat snorted as she put the car in gear with only a little grinding of the transmission.

"'Course I did. I may be scatterbrained sometimes, but damned if I'm gonna go through everything we went through tonight and not have a single thing to show for it in the end. Or leave something like a gun laying around for the cops to find."

Tansy turned as carefully as she could when the car jerked into motion with a spray of gravels, trying to keep an eye on the old shack. But between the billow of smoke from Cat's car and the dim taillights, she couldn't see a thing.

The faint pink wash of morning above the ridge line wasn't going to light much on the ground for a while yet.

If they weren't off the road and out of sight by then, they'd have a whole new set of problems to worry about.

"Shit, there it is." Cat backed off full-speed-ahead around one of the road's many twists and turns. "Looks like she wasn't anywhere near as smart as you were worried about with where she parked. That was a damn good idea you had about blocking our way out of here."

A medium-sized blue Ford was parked off to the side and all the way out of the road. One of those new models that looked like a cross between a sedan and an SUV.

In other words, nothing Vickie would have been able to afford in this lifetime.

"I imagine she thought she'd deal with us quick and easy enough that we wouldn't be driving ourselves when she was done," Tansy said. "At least whoever she *borrowed* it from should get it back in one piece, since she won't be driving it anymore."

Cat sped back up to on-the-screaming-edge-of fast enough to lose control in the gravels. The engine roared loud enough that she had to raise her voice to a near-shout.

"Why'd she do it, do you think? Follow us out there. Sounded to me like she didn't know about the museum until she jumped me and grabbed that mandolin."

"She always was a mean one," Tansy said. "I wasn't the only one in the family to think she lived and breathed nothing but pure bitter spite half the time. Not even that she was jealous, though she sure was that. It was more like she didn't want anyone else to have anything that might make them happy or satisfied at all. Most of the things she got herself into trouble over was what she considered getting even, but no one ever knew what for. I never could figure her out."

"Most I ever did was try to stay clear of her. But I still heard her carrying on about buying that old barn of a house you mentioned, shoveling one load of crap after another. There was this one time—"

"Did you see that?" Tansy jumped in. "That blue flash up there, on the hillside?"

Cat stared long enough that she had to jerk the wheel at the next curve, skidding them an uncomfortably long way toward the thick stands of pine trees on the side of the road.

It didn't much matter whether she'd seen the lights or not.

Tansy knew what they meant.

"Didn't see it, too busy watching the road," Cat said as she accelerated again from scary fast to heart-stopping fast. "You think that's the cops headed this way?"

"I wish I could say I think that. There's no other reason on earth for that color out here this time of night. We might have finally pushed our luck too far, Cat."

Instead of getting upset or even angry, Cat only laughed. Not her high-pitched little girl laugh, not this time.

Now she sounded like a grown-ass woman having the time of her life.

"I know we ain't seen much of each other since school, Tansy. But if you think I'm just gonna pull over and politely hold my wrists out like a good little citizen, you don't know the first thing about me. Might want to buckle up."

Tansy hadn't even realized she'd missed that step when she pretty much collapsed into the seat. She fixed it right quick and got a good grip on the door handle for good measure.

"What are you planning to do?"

Cat whipped through another set of curves, somehow steering her ancient rattletrap through on the closest thing to a straight line.

"Well, I figure odds are any halfway good cops heading out on this call have to be coming from Estonoa. That's where most of the county ones are based. I sure as hell doubt anyone else has been out on all these old mining roads besides you and me for a long stretch of years, so we got a big advantage."

An image of Cat staring at a huge, gritty survey map of the mine's property flashed into Tansy's head. She'd been too busy focusing on the tunnels and shafts under the ground and how they lined up with the museum to pay much attention to the surface.

But Cat had.

"You know all the back roads, don't you?"

Cat grinned and made a clicking noise with her tongue.

"You might could say that. Drove 'em too, before you showed up and again while you were out on your innocent little shopping trip. And if I get us out of here and back to the blacktop fast enough, I got a good chance of getting us out of sight before they make the first turn onto this pitiful excuse for a road. All they'll see is a cloud of dust."

Tansy wasn't sure if the churning in her belly was from fear or hope.

"You think you can beat them?"

This time Cat snorted and shook her head without ever looking away from the stretch of gravel in front of them.

"Guess I have plenty of times before. You best hang on.."

# CHAPTER 19

THE CAR WENT airborne over a rise, neatly avoiding one of the potholes that looked big and mean enough to eat an axle for an early morning snack. Cat's suspension didn't quite bottom out when they crunched back down, but the jounce clacked Tansy's teeth together hard enough to make her head ring.

"What if it's the cops coming from Craigen instead? It's a lot closer."

"Then I guess you and me will be guests of the county for a while, and no worries about paying the bills. But don't go picking out your fancy going-to-court outfit just yet."

Tansy wished she'd been paying a hell of a lot more attention when they drove out to the mine. She'd been too busy going over the Great and Changeable Plan in her head.

That and worrying about everything that could go wrong.

Not that her crystal ball had proved to be worth a damn on that account.

Plenty had gone wrong, or nearly so.

And she hadn't expected any of it.

Now all the planning in the world wouldn't help get them through this last crunch.

Only Cat's complete lack of fear and her skill at threading the needle between police cars and a fiery crash would do the job.

Or not.

"All I got to do, now," Cat sang in a rising and falling tune from some old song Tansy couldn't quite remember, "is get off this road, before they get on it."

Tansy was glad for the grimy seatbelt around her hips and chest when Cat let off the gas.

And ready to show up in church on Sunday and sing hallelujah when a tap on the brakes shoved her forward.

Cat whipped the wheel hard to the right, sending the car skidding sideways.

Apparently aiming for a stack of boulders.

Just as Tansy braced one hand against the cracked dashboard and raised her other arm to cover her face, the headlights jumped from reflecting solid gray rock to pointing into darkness.

A side road she hadn't noticed on the way in.

Cat spun the wheel back and hit the gas at the same time.

Pushing Tansy back against the seat and flying ahead again.

She tried to keep the laugh out of her voice, but didn't quite manage.

"How far does *this* one go?"

"Having fun now, ain't you? This one only goes about a mile, but it gets us right to a crazy tangle up ahead. Roads pointing in five different directions. I heard Uncle Casey say that's all from the old logging days before the mines."

She actually slowed down for a groove across the road from rainwater cutting across, not quite wide enough to capture the tires.

"Is the whole thing in this bad a shape?"

"Naaah. They kept it up pretty good during the pot mine days. Just in case they had to run from the cops just like we are now. Didn't help them none once they blew that electric line."

She sped up again, then slowed as the trees alongside the road thinned out.

Up ahead, Tansy saw the weird intersection that would have been right at home in the snarled streets of the oldest neighborhoods in Atlanta.

The land rose to the right, and two roads branched off that way. A dead end loomed in front of them, but a little further on another road curved out of sight.

Two more branched off to the left.

None of them looked to be in great condition, but they seemed passable.

But Cat wasn't passing anything at all.

The car drifted to a standstill, leaving Tansy's ears echoing in the near-silence.

She leaned over, trying to get a look at the heat gauge.

"Calm yourself down, Tansy. She's not overheated or out of gas or anything else. Just giving the dust a chance to settle."

"The dust they might follow right straight to us, you mean?"

For the first time since they'd left the unpleasant burial site for Vickie behind, Cat turned and looked Tansy in the eye.

In the greenish glow from the dashboard, Cat's whole face showed a fierce, infectious joy.

"They might at that. But if we sit here just a minute, they won't be able to see where we went."

Instead of taking one of the left-hand roads like Tansy expected, Cat rolled slowly across to the one that went straight ahead.

Not a trace of dust stirred up behind them as they went.

And the cloud from their passage was already drifting away in all directions.

"I can't exactly creep along like this all the way back to town," Cat said. "But we'll be out of sight here in just a couple seconds. Then it's a clean shot to the other side of town."

Tansy rubbed her eyes, trying to get herself oriented after so many years of living away.

"I don't see how you're gonna do that, Cat. No way this little spur road loops all the way back around like that. Once they find Vickie, they're sure to set up roadblocks on the highway."

Cat nodded, speeding up to what must seem slow to her, but was almost a sensible speed for a forgotten backwoods gravel road.

"Yeah, I reckon they'll set up roadblocks. But I'd say that will take them a little while, and they'll concentrate on the main roads. Thing is, this ain't nowhere near the only backroad I got tucked away inside my head. I expect we might get through this thing yet."

Tansy decided more questions would only distract Cat and the organic road atlas she apparently kept between her ears. So she got as comfortable as she could with her shoulder deciding to throb now instead of ache.

Even paying as close attention as she could to all the turns Cat took, Tansy knew she wouldn't have a chance in hell of retracing where they'd been.

With only a quick jaunt along the still-clear highway to get to another abandoned-looking dirt road on the other side, they ended up rolling back into town about an hour later.

With no trace of a police car in sight.

And the yellow light of sunrise peeking over the edge of the ridge line that circled Craigen.

By the time Cat killed the engine and let out a long, slow breath, Tansy's back and the cut on her side had taken up the complaining along with her shoulder.

"That was some damn fine driving, Cat."

Cat smacked the steering wheel and nodded.

"Can't find a thing in the world to argue in what you just said. That's the most fun I've *had* driving in way too damn long. I figure we earned us a good rest after all that nonsense." She paused for a second, watching Tansy and obviously trying not to smile. "After we haul all this stuff inside, that is."

Much as Tansy's whole body was taking up the ache and fussing, she hauled herself out of the seat with a groan.

A wispy, early morning springtime fog decorated the whole town, probably only for a couple of hours. Then it would sink back down into the Clinch River where it came from. Thick enough to muffle sounds and hide most of the ridge line, but not so much that she and Cat didn't need to get themselves and everything else out of sight.

The not-exactly-pleasant aroma of the car's big oil-burner

of an engine hung too heavy for the fresh smell of the fog to drive away.

Cat's apartment was in an ordinary red-brick building, not much different from several around town. A little grimy around the grout lines, maybe, and the single-pane windows had to be at least the same age as the World War II memorial statue in the town park. But not terrible when it came to cheap housing without too many questions asked.

Thankfully her place was on the ground floor instead of up two or three of the narrow flights of black metal stairs that spidered along the sides.

"You got somewhere in mind to hide everything?" Tansy said, "In case Vail County's finest get it into their heads to start searching door to door?"

Tansy felt a little bit better about her body's nonstop bitching when Cat lifted her own backpack out of the back seat with a grunt.

"Not that I expect them to come pounding on my door anytime soon, but I got a couple of stashes no one's ever caught on to. Come on, let's get our stove-in asses inside before we both fall down."

# CHAPTER 20

TANSY STARTLED awake at a flat-out awful shrieking noise right beside her ear.

Her drowsy mind was convinced she'd fallen asleep in that triple-damned pot mine, and the racket was the roof in the middle of a slow-motion collapse.

Probably because she'd been caught in an uneasy dream about Vickie digging her way out, by her bloody fingernails, all the way under the earth until she blew a hole in Cat's apartment floor with nothing but the horrible sound of her repeated, furious screams.

An all-over-her-body feeling of sweat and grittiness made an explosion of dirt from a revenge-driven demon of a cousin seem realistic enough.

Several of her pounding heartbeats passed before she realized the noise was her cell phone, and a few more seconds of cussing about forgetting to silence the wretched thing before she managed to focus enough to answer it.

Keeping her eyes squeezed closed during the whole operation was the only choice that made any sense.

Her reward for a muttered greeting was a woman's voice thick with tears.

"Tansy honey? Is that you?"

Doing her best to keep from sounding like she'd been laying out all night drunk instead of running around underground thieving, Tansy cleared her tight and scratchy throat before she answered.

The foul, sour taste in her mouth would have fit right in with a drinking binge. But the feeling of dirt coating her tongue and teeth only made sense with the questionable activities of the night before, plus being too exhausted to brush before she collapsed.

"Yeah, it's me. Is that you, Auntie Louise?"

A mighty sniff and a long, dramatic sigh on the other end of the cell phone let her know before another word was spoken.

"It sure is, honey, and I've got some awful bad news. I hate to tell you something like this over the phone. But I don't want you to hear about it out in town first. It's about your cousin."

Tansy froze, realizing she hadn't given one solitary second of thought to what to say right now. Even though her always kind-hearted Auntie Louise was the most likely in the whole family to feel bad about Vickie's fate, and to think to let Tansy know.

And besides dealing with a wave of guilt so thick and bitter it made her head throb, Tansy was too worn out to make decisions on the fly.

The half-moan when she sat up was real, with both her

wrenched shoulder and the bricklike cushions of Cat's ancient couch forcing it through her now achy throat. She held the phone away when she grunted at the sharp catch and pull as the movement probably tore loose the fragile scabs fighting to keep the long slice on her side from constantly oozing.

Smearing the wound with half a tube of not-quite-expired antibiotic ointment Cat had stashed in her coffin-sized bathroom didn't give nearly enough pain relief hours later. At least the thick wads of gauze Tansy wound around herself kept the blood from getting out.

So far.

Her mind felt almost as rough as the fabric that went right through the cheap, thin sheet under her legs and backside. The room had been too stuffy and hot to stand another sheet all night long.

Opening her eyes to the sorry reality of the bland, almost empty living room wouldn't make any of that better, so she decided not to.

Tansy managed to keep herself from mentioning Vickie's name, but it was a close call.

"I'm here, Auntie Louise. Which cousin? What's going on?"

That world-class sigh again, and a sob that sounded all too real.

"Well, I'm sorry to say poor little Vickie's troubles caught up with her at last. She's gone, honey. She's passed away."

No one in the family, not even Auntie Louise, had any kind of delusions that Tansy and Vickie cared much for each other, or even got along. But a shrug would never be the right response to news like this.

"Oh no. What happened?"

"I don't rightly know yet, honey. Seems the police are in the thick of it now, or I should say the sheriff is because they found her outside of town. But you know as well as I do it's not too much of a surprise with that poor girl. She never did make it easy to care for her, bless her heart. Never much learned to care for herself either."

Tansy finally opened one eye, afraid the stab of morning sunlight through Cat's yellowish yard sale lace curtains would be too much to face with both of them. Thankfully a tolerable glow that looked more like afternoon let her know she'd at least gotten a fair amount of sleep.

"Did they... I'm real sorry to hear that, Auntie Louise. Do they know what happened to her?"

"I don't doubt somebody does, but they're too damn cowardly to show their murdering faces." Auntie Louise rarely got angry, but no one misunderstood when she did. "I'm real sorry to snap at you like that, honey. I'm just tore all to pieces over this."

Tansy rubbed her temples, fighting back the unpleasant urge to confess the whole thing right then and there. Of all the people to call her, Auntie Louise was surely the most likely and most obvious.

But she was the worst person too, by a long shot. Because she was well and truly upset about Vickie's death. More than anyone else in the family or anywhere in the whole county was likely to be.

"You don't have to identify the...identify her, do you?"

Again that well-practiced sigh. And this time it just about broke Tansy's heart.

"No, thank the Good Lord I don't have to do that.

Someone else already did. I reckon someone down at her job knew to call me and told the sheriff, even though she's been staying out at that one-room rental place on Bonny Hill. Guess they'd call it a fancy studio apartment in some big city, but I just call it highway robbery from those that can least afford to pay it. Don't know when we'll get to have a funeral for her, since they have to do the investigation and all."

Of course they'd call Auntie Louise, and Tansy doubted very much that the police had to ask anyone about it. Vickie had been fetching up at Auntie Louise's warm, friendly house after her latest run-in with the law for decades.

"I wish there was something I could do, Auntie Louise. I'm real sorry to hear about Vickie. Are you okay?"

Cat chose that moment to stumble into the living room, wearing a faded brown Dale Earnhardt NASCAR t-shirt and a pair of denim shorts cut off so short the white pockets hung down against her pale thighs. When Tansy pointed to the phone clutched against her ear, Cat nodded and just about fell into a threadbare chair that matched the sofa.

"I'm doing all right considering what's happened," Auntie Louise said. "Seems I've been worried about Vickie for so long I flat don't know what to do with myself now. Listen honey, the sheriff might want to talk to you. When they spoke to the people where Vickie was working, they said she got herself all worked up the other day, enough so they worried enough to talk to her parole officer about it. Someone said you were in there right before she got so upset."

The lightning strike of fear must have shown through loud and clear on Tansy's face. Cat leaned forward in her chair.

"What's wrong?" she whispered.

"I was in there, yeah." Tansy hoped her voice wasn't shaking as much as she was. "I sure didn't mean to upset her if I did. I had no idea she was working there until I walked in. Did the sheriff say what they want to talk to me about?"

Cat covered her mouth with both hands, and Tansy nodded.

"Oh no, honey, you didn't do anything wrong at all. I didn't mean to make it sound that way. It's just that they're trying to figure out who Vickie might have been with yesterday, or last night, I guess. They just want to talk to folks who saw her last is all. I got the feeling they're hoping that can help them put together who did this terrible thing."

Tansy hated to drag her sweet auntie into this mess even more than she hated to stir up the sickening tangle of guilt that was making her stomach churn.

But the more she knew before she was staring down someone from the sheriff's office, the better.

"It sounds to me like you think someone hurt Vickie. Is that what they told you?"

"Well, not in so many words, no. All they said was they thought someone else must have been there from the way things looked where...where they found her. I hadn't heard her say a word about anyone new, but you know how she had a way of keeping herself to herself when it suited her. I figure she took up with the worst person for her like she always seemed to do."

# CHAPTER 21

PRICKLY, uncomfortable chills made Tansy's skin feel as rough as the couch cushions.

Her auntie didn't know what had really happened, and probably never would have suspected it. And Vickie hadn't *taken up* with Tansy one time since they first laid eyes on each other as little girls.

But following Tansy down to that triple-damned pot mine had been the last of Vickie's many bad decisions.

"I only saw her for that minute or two down at the farm supply, but I'll help if I can. Everyone else okay? Do you need anything?"

Auntie Louise snorted, loosening the heavy clamp of shame closing in on Tansy's heart a tiny bit.

"Lord, honey, I could talk your ear plumb off with a list of things I'd *like* to say I need. I guess most of all is going to be the patience to deal with everyone else in the family, trying to pretend like they always worried so and did their level best for that poor child. You know I love them, but they'll put a lot more work into nasty gossip now then they ever did trying to help Vickie when it might have possibly made a difference for her."

Tansy shook her head, unwilling to pretend she'd been any different. And thankful a thousand times over that her auntie couldn't get a good look at her face.

"I'm real sorry, Auntie Louise. You always did your best to help Vickie, everyone knows that. You just give me a call if I can do anything for you, hear me?"

"I'll tell you what you can do, and what you *better* do. I got no idea when we can have the wake or the funeral or the burial. But you better get yourself over here to see me before you head back to wherever you're living these days. Don't make me come after you, now."

"I wouldn't dare leave without seeing you, Auntie Louise. And that's a promise."

When Tansy ended the call—hoping with all her might that the funeral would be delayed long enough that she could be long gone—Cat stared at her, both hands gripping her bruised knees.

"They already found her?"

Tansy filled her lungs long and slow, then let her smelly morning breath out through pursed lips before she answered

"Found her long enough ago that they're already talking to people down at the farm supply and my Auntie Louise. If you want the truth, I'm sure they were on the spot before you got us back to town."

Cat shivered and wrapped her arms around herself.

"The ones coming from the museum and driving up the road probably met right in the middle. I figured they were both there. I guess I tried to believe it would take them longer to start poking around. What are you going to tell them, Tansy?"

"Not a single thing they don't directly ask me, and as little as I can of that. The only thing we got to work out is what we were doing last night. I figure from the way my breath stinks and my head feels, we put away enough Jack and Coke to give five burly high school football players a nasty hangover."

Cat nodded slowly, scrubbing one hand through her smushed up (but cobweb free) hair.

"Spending the whole night watching trashy movies from the 90s was enough to give me a hangover. Give me a minute to fetch the Bloody Mary mix I keep for emergencies like this one, and we'll be all set so you can invite the cops on over."

She stood, and the angle of afternoon light coming in the window highlighted the bruises and swelling on her face. Besides the busted lip, she had the start of a vivid black eye.

"You look beat to shit, Cat. Probably better if I go to them. You know, volunteer before I get that extra-special invitation. I'll just tell them Auntie Louise passed the word to me when she called. Your story makes sense to me, so be ready if they call to check it out. I will take some of that Bloody Mary mix, though. My stomach isn't exactly settled right now."

After a couple of seconds of scowling, Cat nodded.

"Fine by me. Fits a lot of what happened anyway. I ran into you down by the river and we decided to get together for old time's sake. If whoever you talk to is anywhere near our age, they'll remember the old times we'd be celebrating."

She started toward the tiny kitchen, then stopped.

"I guess it's a good thing I didn't get any buyers lined up after all. We'll have to wait until things cool down a little."

Tansy stared up at the white popcorn-patterned ceiling, an unfortunate relic from at least forty years before.

"Yeah, it's a *damn* good thing as it turns out. We won't be talking to any sellers, Cat. Not anywhere around here, or anywhere else for a good long time. Not with a dead person that looks an awful lot like a murder mixed up in this whole business. The cops will be watching out for any word of the stuff that went missing, way more than they would have for a simple robbery. Everything changed when Vickie showed up."

Cat opened her mouth, brow creased, and stopped. Her face and her whole body seemed to slump in slow motion.

"We can't do *anything* with the stuff, can we? We're stuck with it all. Every last bit of the whole mess was for not a damn thing in the end."

Tansy winced, thinking of her Auntie Louise's heartbroken voice. Seeing her in person was going to be even worse.

For once, Cat's casual disregard for consequences was too much to deal with.

"It all turned sour right then, yes. When someone *died*. Much as I never got along with Vickie, I never would have wanted this to happen. And not just because you're right. We're stuck with it all. For now. Might be able to move it way off in the future, and nowhere near here. We just have to get through the next few days, maybe a couple of weeks. Not the best time for me to suddenly take off, either. If they got a good look at the museum's security tapes, they'll surely know I was there the other day on top of people seeing me at the farm supply."

Cat looked down at her hands knotted together against her belly, then walked back to her chair and sat.

"I didn't want that to happen either, to you or to Vickie. Hell Tansy, I'm real sorry about dragging you into this. I know the last thing you wanted was to get stuck here after you already got away."

Tansy smacked her thighs and got slowly to her feet. Her body was achy and sore enough to have gone on a bender, too, and she probably had at least as many new bruises decorating her skin as Cat did.

"Come on, Cat. We might not have been in touch for a long damn time, but you know me better than that. When have I ever done something I didn't decide to do on my own? Outside of school I mean, and even then it was doubtful."

Cat looked up with a trace of a smile.

"I guess you got a point there. Stubborn as hell and twice as ornery. You're welcome here long as you want to stay, not that it's exactly comfortable sleeping. I was gonna get rid of that old ratty couch with the money, pitiful as that sounds."

"Doesn't sound pitiful to me at all. It *is* like sleeping on a stack of bricks." Tansy winked. "Don't write the whole thing off just yet. Our plans might have gotten busted all to hell, but I know we can think of something. Let's go scrounge up something to eat and figure out what rotten movies we got drunk to last night, so I can to talk to the cops before they charge in here hunting for me."

Cat rolled her eyes as she stood beside Tansy.

"Already told you no one ever finds my stash. But you scrub your nasty ass and get yourself all dolled up before you go pay them a visit. Keeps me from having to try and prettify my own self when it's more of a struggle than usual. When you get back, we'll get ourselves to work figuring out what the hell we're going to do next."

"I'll do my best, but it might take a whole lot of doing, beat as I am." She raised the old white t-shirt she'd fallen asleep in, not surprised to see red spots blooming across the wad of gauze. "Biggest challenge might be keeping blood from seeping through all over the place. Hey, where's my gun? And I never did see what you did with my jacket and that shirt from the museum. They're not with the rest of the stuff, are they?"

Cat grinned and pointed to an old iron heater grate in the floor.

"Surely you noticed how hot it is in here? I meant to tell you to crack the window but forgot. This old building ain't much to look at, but it's got a real handy bonus down in the basement. I guess my neighbors will be working overtime trying to figure out who cranked the boiler up for more than hot water so late in the spring. That jacket and mine and your floor-mopping shirt won't be nothing but ashes by now. And your gun is safe and sound with the gold record and all the rest."

Tansy shook her head and smiled, surprised yet again at how many tricks Cat had up her sleeve.

"I thought I saw a little furnace out there in the kitchen. In that closet where you keep your pantry stuff?"

Cat snorted and waved one hand.

"Yeah, that was one of the landlord's great big ideas a couple of years back. Quit fixing the boiler and push more of the cost for heat and hot water off on us. You know, so we could adjust it however we want to, not that she was going to lower rent or anything like that. She got nothing but bitching about the whole idea. That and a nasty surprise about how much redoing the plumbing would cost since she couldn't get one of her crooked friends to do it cut-rate like she did the furnaces. Still got those ugly things sitting around because she's too cheap to get 'em hauled off."

Cat pursed her lips and knotted her hands together.

"Listen Tansy, I somehow manage not to spend too much time talking to the cops, despite some of my hobbies. But don't you need a lawyer or something like that to keep you from saying the wrong things?"

Tansy rubbed her cheek, a little grossed out at how grubby her skin felt even after she'd done her best to wash all the blood and dust and grime off without taking a shower and risking getting dirty water and soap into the cut.

"Even if I could afford one, I'm afraid if I go strutting in there with a fancy lawyer in tow, they'll decide right then and there that I must have something worth hiding. If they decide to make me a guest of the county and *encourage* me to stay a while, I figure that's the time to bring in the professionals."

Cat tilted her head to the side, no doubt thinking it over.

"Whatever you say. Don't invite them over for a beer or anything, but don't worry. They'd have to take the whole building down to find the stuff. My money says they'd miss it even then."

Tansy couldn't argue about the hiding place, since she had no idea where it was herself. Cat had insisted on moving everything out of the living room without help, and Tansy had been too tired to stay up and argue.

Much as she didn't love the idea of walking into the police

station, especially with a bunch of sheriff's department folks in town, that was still better than trusting their luck if the cops showed up at Cat's place.

That luck might still be holding out so far—at least for the two of them—but Tansy had no doubt it was hanging on by a thread thinner than a spiderweb.

# CHAPTER 22

TANSY KNEW things were a hell of a lot worse than she imagined before she parked at the tiny little police department in Craigen.

Partly because there wasn't a single parking space to be had anywhere near the squat brown brick building. That by itself was unusual enough to get one-hundred percent of her attention on an ordinary weekday afternoon.

Most of the time, only a couple of gray and blue patrol cruisers sat nosed in around the blacktop parking lot or idling right out front.

Today the lot was jammed full, and both sides of the street in front were nose-to-tail a couple of blocks down. Not full of Vail County's shit-brown vehicles, either, though several more of them than usual dotted the vehicular landscape.

Tansy spotted cars and SUVs from three neighboring counties, police from several little towns nearby, and even a handful of silver and blue Virginia State Troopers—almost as rare a sighting in rural Craigen as black limousines carrying state or federal officials who finally remembered the tail end of the state existed.

Way more regular cars and trucks were overflowing from the sheriff's office and along the side streets, too. Tansy would have bet what looked like unusual crowds parked around the beauty salon, barbecue joint, discount tobacco outlet, and churches within walking distance were sardined inside with all the law enforcement instead.

Either there'd been some other kind of notorious crime overnight, or Captain O'Quinn and the Confederates had a way more dedicated fanbase than she expected.

She'd just about decided to drive back to Cat's apartment and walk the mile or so back when she finally found a spot behind the post office a couple of blocks away. Probably only because she remembered sneaking back there to make out with some boy or other when she was in high school. Likely most people had no idea the space was there, or it would have been full.

The day had come up bright and sunny, reclaiming May with a preview of summer's heat on the breeze. But that wasn't the real reason Tansy was afraid she'd sweat right through her green blouse and blue slacks—an outfit she'd only packed in case someone decided to drag her to church.

All those people crowded into their little town for no good reason couldn't possibly be a good thing for her, or for Cat. If nothing else, there'd be a whole lot more eyes and ears listening in to try to catch her in a lie.

The worst part was the salt from her sweat doing every-thing it could to remind her of all the rough activities of the night before, especially when it seeped into the still-open cut on her side.

She'd re-covered it with a downright paranoid amount of antibiotic gel Cat retrieved from the same kitchen cabinet as all those rubber gloves, too grateful for the huge selection of wound-care supplies to ask questions about why so much was there in the first place. Then layered on enough gauze and medical tape that the bulge would have shown under something as close-fitting as a t-shirt.

But keeping the deepest wound protected didn't help with the startling number of smaller scrapes and scratches Tansy had managed to pick up with so much scrabbling around. On her knees and hands, her back and arms, even the back of her head.

Without those stinging reminders, she might still be standing under the too-hot spray in the shower, tilted to one side in an attempt to keep burning soap out of the big cut, letting the water do its best to work out the awful cramps and soreness that had spread from her shoulder across her back and even around to her abdomen.

Stepping inside the building didn't do a thing to calm her nerves, dry her damp palms, or slow her racing heart.

Tan and burgundy and different shades of blue uniforms stood around in little groups everywhere. Crowded around desks, leaning against walls, blocking the narrow hallways.

The stink of overcooked cheap coffee was almost enough to make her gag even before the thick undertone of too much perspiration under polyester took over.

The shrill ring of old-fashioned black desk phones cut through the roar of too many people talking at the same time over and over again, making Tansy clench her fists to keep from running right back out of there.

If she had somewhere reasonable to run to—and if she hadn't told her Auntie Louise she'd talk to the police—she would have done just that.

A red-faced kid who had to be twenty years younger than her walked toward the front door, carrying a white cardboard box. He wore a blue uniform she didn't recognize, and she hoped his scowl didn't mean he recognized her.

"Can I help you, ma'am?"

"I'm here to... Someone here wants to talk to me? About what happened last night."

He jerked his chin toward his left shoulder.

"See Deputy Salyers, she's handling the interviews. Second desk, against the wall."

Tansy nodded, but she couldn't get her feet to move.

That name set off an alarm bell in her mind, one she couldn't match with a thought just yet.

Not the countdown alarm that lit up her brain sometimes, either. The kind she could get herself away from with quick thinking or removing herself from the situation.

This was more like a fire alarm going off about six inches away from her ear.

The man in front of her sighed and shook his head.

"She's right over there, ma'am. Can I maybe get around you, please?"

Tansy stared at him for a second, until the uproar in her mind finally managed to get a handle on what he said.

"Oh, I'm sorry. Thank you for your help."

She stepped to the side enough to let him get out the door, but she still didn't head toward Deputy Salyers.

Tansy knew the longer she stood there, the more likely someone else would notice her even with so much more activity than this little town normally saw.

But the insistent feeling that she needed to remember who this Deputy Salyers was before she went over there kept her frozen in place.

She leaned forward enough to peer through the crowd and see who was behind the second desk against the wall.

The African-American woman in the dark-blue uniform looked somewhere in the neighborhood of thirty, with buzz-cut hair and a face that seemed too friendly for a cop. She leaned forward with her elbows on her cluttered wooden desk, talking to one of the state troopers dressed in pale gray. From the way they both gestured and nodded, the conversation surely had to be too important to interrupt for a random cousin-of-the-victim's little interview.

For once in her life, Tansy resisted the urge to take the easy excuse and leave.

She wanted to do her best to keep herself and Cat out of trouble, sure. And she didn't want to admit to her Auntie Louise that she'd broken her word.

What she didn't expect was an overwhelming sense of owing this to Vickie somehow. Maybe having the courage to walk over there and sit down in front of Deputy Salyers would let her cousin rest easier.

And let Tansy rest easier, too.

Both officers stopped talking and looked up at her before

she made it halfway across the room with a careful stride she hoped didn't make it obvious how sore her body was.

"Excuse me, Deputy Salyers? You're doing the interviews about Vickie Stidham?"

Deputy Salyers nodded, not looking close to as friendly as she did before. The state trooper got up, touched two fingers to his forehead in a brief salute, and disappeared into the crowd.

"Have a seat. And tell me who you are and what brought you into the madhouse today."

Tansy's breath seized into a solid, gunky mass inside her throat and chest.

Because she finally knew where she'd heard Deputy Salyers' name before, and her voice.

Drifting down the dusty, cobweb-infested stairs of the Country on the Clinch Music Museum and Gallery, while Tansy huddled in the corner of the basement and Cat did the same in the pot mine below.

Tansy had never been much of a believer in fate and karma and whatever they preached down at the Baptist Church where so many of her relatives spent pretty much every hour of their spare time.

But sitting face-to-face with the deputy who'd come so close to catching her and Cat gave her confidence a good, hard shove.

She cleared her throat a couple of times, hoping her voice would come out normal.

"Tansy Stidham, ma'am. I'm Vickie's cousin. My aunt called to tell me what happened to her, and said you might want to talk to me."

Deputy Salyers raised her fine eyebrows, then looked down at an electronic tablet on her desk.

"Tansy. The one who dropped by the farm supply a few days ago, right?"

Tansy only nodded, not sure what she could say without the conversation turning to what she bought that day, and why.

Deputy Salyers nodded. "From what I heard, your cousin got pretty upset while you were in there. Enough so people noticed. Any idea why she might have reacted that way? Did the two of you talk to each other?"

"No ma'am, we didn't say a word. I... Well, I could see she wasn't happy about me being there, so I kept moving."

"Not being happy is one way to put it, since she acted up enough to lose her job. Which got her parole officer pretty unhappy, too." Deputy Salyers looked completely calm, but the words hit Tansy like a kick to the gut. "Some kind of history between you two that might cause her to do that?"

Tansy took a quick breath and folded her damp hands together so she wouldn't start cracking her knuckles. All the noise in the sheriff's office had dropped to a dull roar in her ears.

"We never did get along if that's what you're asking. I mean, Vickie kind of has...*had* a hard time getting along with a lot of people. But some folks in the family tried real hard to stay on her good side. I guess I didn't much bother to try."

Deputy Salyers grabbed a very old-fashioned yellow pencil from the piles of paper and folders on her desk and tapped the eraser end against the tablet's glowing screen.

"I had a few run-ins with Vickie myself, so I understand

why you might feel that way. What seems strange to me is her parole officer was pretty surprised by what happened. Seems like she'd been doing really well for a few weeks. Better than usual. Then just the sight of you set her off, she got herself fired, and next thing we know, she turns up dead. I may be chasing my tail here, but I'm just wondering if there's not a connection I haven't figured out yet."

Tansy forced herself to keep looking into Deputy Salyers' brown eyes, but not to stare and make it obvious how much she wanted to look away.

She wasn't quite sure why her being there set Vickie off so badly, and the truth was no one besides Vickie would ever know.

But now she had an uncomfortably clear idea why Vickie followed her and Cat out to the mine. And why she'd been so angry.

Losing a badly needed job could do that to a person.

And that was the reaction that sent Vickie to her awful end a lot farther under the ground than the typical six feet.

"Not that I know of, ma'am. It's been a few years since I spent much time here, so maybe she was surprised to see me is all I can think of. Only other thing I could guess is she got extra mad at me because I moved away instead of sitting right here like she did."

"What brought you back? Anything special?"

"Nothing special, besides thinking it was probably time I visited home."

Deputy Salyers was silent for what felt like an hour, still tapping the eraser on her tablet.

"How'd you enjoy our new museum?"

Even though Tansy figured they'd know about that by now, the question still startled her.

But if she'd seen all those tapes and hadn't matched daytime-Tansy up with the one who did the stealing, that had to be a good thing.

"I think they did a real nice job getting it set up, and the guide was friendly as he could be. Does he keep a list of everyone who stops by or something?"

"If he keeps a list I haven't seen it yet. I was just reviewing the security footage a couple of hours ago and recognized your face. Did your aunt mention they had a robbery there last night?"

Tansy scowled and shook her head.

"She sure didn't. I hope it wasn't too bad. You think that's tied up with whatever happened to Vickie?"

Deputy Salyers dropped the pencil and sat back, watching Tansy.

"Could be. Mind if I ask what you were doing last night?"

"I don't mind at all. Me and Cat Maybell got to catching up and watching old movies, ended up drinking a little bit more than I meant to. So I stayed over there."

The chatter in the office cut off all at once, and both Tansy and Deputy Salyers turned.

A woman who didn't look like anyone there—or from anywhere in Vail County—stood right inside the front door. She was tall and striking, with honey-blonde hair streaked with silver falling long and wavy over her shoulders and diamond earrings that sparkled too much to be fake. Her shimmery black jacket and pants looked like they cost more than Tansy's car, maybe more than when it was brand new.

Her green eyes were too red and puffy for her perfect makeup to hide, but her sharp intelligence still somehow lit the overcrowded room.

Tansy couldn't begin to guess her age, even though she'd made no attempt to hide lines around her mouth, eyes, and forehead. The rest of her skin was still smooth and healthy enough that she might be anywhere from forty to eighty.

"Thank you for your time, Miss Stidham," Deputy Salyers said in a low voice as people started talking again. Quietly. "Let me get your phone number in case I have any more questions. And if you think of anything else you want to tell me about, give me a call."

She handed over a white business card with little black print on one side, then tapped Tansy's number into her tablet. When she stood, her attention plainly on the woman who'd quieted the whole room just by showing her face, Tansy stood as well.

"Okay then," Tansy said. "You're welcome, Deputy Salyers."

She forced herself to walk slowly toward the door instead of getting as close as she could to a sprint. But she didn't want to go near the woman still waiting like a flawless statue that got lost in the middle of Nowhere, Appalachia, when she meant to aim toward the fancy side of a big city.

The woman's green eyes followed Tansy, feeling like laser beams meant to scorch her alive.

At the last second, she stepped aside, but didn't look away from Tansy.

Without understanding why, Tansy ducked her head in a brief nod and darted out the door.

She walked as fast as she could back toward the post office, not caring now if she sweated right through her clothes. Getting herself away from the zoo in the sheriff's office—and while Deputy Salyers was still too distracted to ask much harder questions—was the only thing that mattered.

By the time Tansy got back to her car, her natural curiosity had kicked in a lot stronger than her urge to run. She had too many questions to even put into words, and most of them were way too important to her and Cat's continued freedom from jail to ignore.

She could only think of one place where it would be safe to ask, and where she'd probably get even more information than all those cops had managed.

Time to head over to the same convenience store she'd stopped by when she first got to Craigen, the day Cat Maybell caught her tossing an empty bottle of water toward the trashcan by the Clinch River.

If anyone in all of Vail County would know the story on the huge crowd at the sheriff's office and the mysterious woman who'd interrupted Deputy Salyers, Tim Calloway and Mark Morris would.

And most important of all, they'd know if any whispers about who'd really robbed the damn museum were drifting around town.

# CHAPTER 23

THE DROP In and Shop had been on the same corner lot beside the highway out of town since before Tansy was born, and she figured it would last until the last human wandering the Earth needed a pack of cigarettes and a cheap can of beer. The tan metal roof and tan bricks with almost wall-to-wall windows seemed as old as the mountains.

They'd sold every brand of gas available, and spent more than a few years dispensing off-brands that might cause more damage to a vehicle than saving a few pennies could ever be worth.

Yet people couldn't seem to resist stopping by, at least long enough to catch up on the latest happenings around town and do their part to keep the gossip stream running high and hard.

Tansy drove through the lumpy parking lot, doing her best to avoid the round metal plates over the huge gas tanks. A childhood paranoia about somehow falling through never quite left her.

Possibly because she'd seen the plates missing or halfway off too often to ignore.

Not too crowded in the odd hours between lunch and people getting off work for the evening, so only a handful of cars and pickup trucks sat at the bright-blue gas pumps or parked badly near the glass doors. The grubby wooden picnic tables that were probably as old as she was sat empty, with only a random splattering of mystery stains all over the tops to show how many people still ate there despite the stink of gasoline and exhaust.

When she stepped inside, a blast of chilly air welcomed her back, full of the familiar aromas of strong coffee, hot dogs and sausages rolling under reddish heat lamps, and frying potato wedges.

A knot of old men in scruffy baseball caps stood by the wall of beer and soda coolers, heads together and hands waving to emphasize whatever they were discussing. The display cases full of candy bars, potato chips, and weird things like car parts, pet food, and paper towels were long enough that their voices didn't carry over the low hum of all those coolers.

The two men she wanted to talk to were busy behind the long, cluttered counter on the opposite side of the store.

Tim Calloway was stocking a new supply of at least a dozen different scratch-off lottery cards, his curly hair too long and getting close to half gray. Mark Morris stood on a step ladder, arranging packs of cigarettes in an overhead case only people behind the counter could see. His blond hair had retreated to sort of a fuzzy skirt around the edges of his head.

Both wore old jeans and t-shirts under blue vests the same

color as the gas pumps outside. And both of them saw Tansy at the same time and waved.

"Hey there, stranger." Mark got down from the ladder with a grunt. "How's your big homecoming going?"

Tansy leaned her elbows on the high fake woodgrain counter, in one of the matched pairs of faded spots where hundreds of locals had done the same for years.

"Pretty much about the way I expected. Which means I'm either too drunk for someone my age, hung over, or about bored out of my skull. Usually two of those at the same time. Anything new and exciting going on around here I should know about?"

Mark widened his eyes. "I'm going to assume you're kidding, because otherwise where the hell have you *been?* Only about the biggest bunch of scandal to hit Craigen in about fifty years. And with one of your cousins right in the middle of the whole thing."

Tansy sighed and shook her head. "Yeah, I got the call about Vickie this morning, but I don't know much of anything about it. Couldn't hardly focus with the morning-after-party headache. Anyway, you know how it goes. The cops said enough to get my poor sweet auntie in an uproar, but didn't say near enough to let on what really happened. I saw a huge crowd at the police station on the way over here, too."

"You'd think they'd get better about how to make folks feel better instead of worse on those calls," Mark said. "Or maybe they could use some of our tax dollars to hire a PR firm instead of setting up speed traps every other day." He raised up on his tiptoes and peered toward the men by the cooler, then leaned closer to Tansy. "Word is they found her inside an old coal mine. The one they grew pot in a bunch of years back."

"I remember hearing about that pot mine." Tansy frowned and shook her head, not needing to fake feeling upset about the whole thing. "They wouldn't even tell my aunt that much, and she's got herself all tore up imagining a whole lot worse. What I can't make sense of is why the hell Vickie would be out there in the first place."

"That's *why* there's such a crowd in town today. They're saying she broke into the new museum if you can believe that." Mark pulled his mouth to one side, a quirk he'd had since high school. "Well, not just her, because someone else was with her. Probably the one that took her out and left her there so they could take off with all the stuff they stole."

"Now that's a damn shame about the museum, too," Tansy said. "I was in there a few days ago. Nice enough setup, but I didn't see anything that would bring half the cops in Vail County swarming into town."

"That all depends on who donated the stuff." Mark lowered his voice. "Your cousin and whoever got away managed to piss off the widow of Captain O'Quinn himself. She's the main reason there's a museum in the first place. Poor thing had to fly all the way from Nashville, and after she swore she'd never set foot in Vail County again after she last visited for the grand opening. Some of her own family got snooty and rude with her. Today she chartered a flight into that scary little airstrip up on the mountain and everything, but I'd bet a month's salary not one of her bitchy kinfolks knew a thing about her visit in advance."

Tansy blinked, trying to imagine how someone from the

same hillbilly clothing and hair background as she was could end up looking as polished and put together as the woman she'd passed in the police station.

"Did Captain O'Quinn make the kind of money that would charter a jet?'

Mark shook his head with a wicked little smile.

"Not with his own music he didn't, and *he* didn't make it at all. At least not while he was alive. Turns out the good Captain left a huge stack of songs he wrote over the years but never got around to recording. And the good Widow O'Quinn knew *exactly* what she had when she found those. She turned right around and sold them to some of the biggest acts in country music."

Tim stepped up behind Mark, brushing his graying curls away from his face.

"Hey there Tansy. What Mark's not telling you is she didn't just *sell* all those songs. She knew enough about how the music business works after years of watching the Confederates never get near as famous as they were good that she figured out how to negotiate. Hard. She made more with those supposedly lost songs than the Captain ever earned from what he recorded."

Mark nodded. "Got a bunch of the old songs re-recorded too, and took home a pretty penny from that part. I hear she's been in the managing game ever since then, helping out younger bands who want to do the same. Teaching folks how to get a bunch of old music back out into the world, too. Word is some of the stuffy Nashville types got their short hairs in a twist over it, but she doesn't give a good god-damn."

"So that's why there's such a crowd in town." Tansy rubbed her eyes, wishing she could stop the thundercloud of a headache gathering directly behind them, as if called into reality by her own lies. "Probably explains all the cops too."

Mark shook his head again. "Not quite all of them. Turns out the getaway car wasn't stolen from some random victim. It belongs to the sheriff's favorite daughter. Everyone in the department was furious that they had to go knock on her door and ask for an alibi. Can you *imagine?*"

Tim nodded, and Tansy could feel them slipping into the tag-team rhythm they'd developed all those years ago when the three of them carried a lot less damage.

"*And* she's a major fundraiser for rural police departments all over the tail-end of Virginia. So that brought in everyone who could cook up a good-enough excuse to head this way. Between those two, I expect the media to hit town any minute now. Probably more than the local news crews from what I'm hearing, because of all the country musicians who know Miz O'Quinn. Most excitement this wide spot in the road has ever seen."

The knot of old men finally finished with their Extremely Important Discussion, and they swarmed the front of the store armed with six-packs of beer, huge bags of chips, and amazingly detailed orders for exactly how they wanted the hot dogs that had surely been spinning under heat lamps for longer than Tansy wanted to think about.

She took herself in the other direction, not wanting one of them to recognize her and start a round of competitive reminiscing about some wild stunt her Daddy pulled years before she was born. One of them looked way too much like an older, meaner version of a guy she remembered seeing a lot when she was a kid.

Besides those kinds of tales being embarrassing and more than a little annoying when someone besides her did the telling, the last thing she needed right now was one motor-mouth gossip in a group full of them remembering just how good her father was at blowing things up.

That was a damn short step to her shopping trip to the farm supply, and the brand-new hole in the museum's basement.

Which neither Mark nor Tim had mentioned, now that she thought about it. She didn't watch half as many of the police shows as Cat apparently did, but she could imagine why that tidbit hadn't made it out into the gossip stream.

Maybe they were trying not to give some other dipshit the same idea.

Or *they* might have an idea who did have the skills and was either brave or stupid enough to do it.

Either way, Tansy didn't like what she was hearing. Not one bit.

# CHAPTER 24

SHE GRABBED a couple of glass bottles of Coke and a huge bag of barbecue potato chips. Partly out of the long-ago habit she and Cat shared of bingeing on them when they were drunk or high or altered in some other unwise way. More because she felt like she should have a reason for stopping in than wanting either one. Then she took her time wandering the aisles to give the baseball cap bunch time to get their extra-special hotdogs and go.

By the time she strolled back to the counter, Mark and Tim were both shaking their heads. The smell of raw onions, mustard, and sweet relish was still strong, and fresh, fleshy pink hotdogs were taking their turn drying out under the orange lamps.

"Cantankerous old coots," Mark said, rolling his eyes. "They come in here almost every day to stand back there and run their mouths for as long as their wives let them get away with it."

"Bet if you asked their wives, they'd tell us to keep them longer," Tim added as he rang up her cover purchases.

"*Then* they tell us the same exact orders they've had for *years* for those smelly shriveled up hotdogs. But they have to repeat everything over and over again, like it's the first time and we just started here yesterday. Never mind that we could get it all ready before they ever walk through the door."

Tansy smiled. "So you're telling me I was right about this town not changing one bit since I left. Until this morning, anyway."

"Ain't that the truth." Mark tilted his head to the side. "Listen, I'm real sorry about Vickie. I never knew her all that well, but she was your cousin."

"She was a tough one to get to know on her good days," Tansy said. "You said she was in that old pot mine, which doesn't surprise me all that much. But what I can't work out is what that has to do with the museum. I've never been out to the mine, but it can't be all that close to town."

Tim snapped his fingers and grinned.

"That is the *very* question everyone rolling through here today keeps asking. I mean, did Vickie's partner in crime lure her out there on purpose? Or did Vickie do the luring, but the whole thing went to hell and she ended up on the wrong end of her own plan?"

Tansy swallowed hard and hoped she didn't look as queasy as she felt.

Even if word of her own blasting handiwork hadn't made it out into the general population yet, Tim had just landed too close to reality to suit her.

"I'm sure you two will puzzle it all out if anyone can." She grabbed the flimsy white plastic bag already chilled from the sodas. "I'll be sure to stop by before I head out of town."

"Yeah you will," Mark said as he climbed back up on his stepladder to finish stocking cigarettes. "Because you can't resist a good puzzle any more than we can."

Tansy waved over her shoulder, already in a hurry to get out of sight and back to the relative shelter of Cat's apartment. At the very least, she'd have someone to talk this whole mess through without worrying about who knew what.

So far only the two of them knew the whole story.

And she intended to keep it that way.

When she finally glanced up to make sure she didn't step into the path of someone in a hurry for a fill up—or in desperate need of their caffeine, nicotine, or sugar fix—she looked directly into the eyes of the man she thought she'd recognized inside.

No way she could pretend he didn't know who she was, either.

He pushed back the bill of his faded orange University of Tennessee cap and scowled down his lumpy nose at her. Something in the set of his thick, grizzled eyebrows and still-sharp blue eyes stirred up memories lost in the fog of years ago.

Couch.

Lee Couch, that was his name.

And he'd been a constant presence around the house when Tansy was a little girl. One of her Daddy's best drinking and general carousing buddies. Lee knew very well what Virge Stidham got up to, because he was right there by his side most of the time.

Until he wasn't.

Try as she might, she couldn't remember what caused the falling out between them, but she knew it had happened. Because all at once, from one day to the next, they'd gone from Virge-and-Lee to Virge-versus-Lee—*and* versus all the rest of the family, including Tansy and her mother—and stayed that way.

Lee never passed a chance to annoy, pester, intimidate, and outright bully them even after her Daddy passed.

She did her best to keep her face from changing at all, focused on the street sign behind him, and kept her feet moving until she got to her car.

Now getting the hell out of sight couldn't happen fast enough.

If she was as smart as she always thought, getting the hell out of town would be her next step. All the loot from the museum be damned.

Assuming she could work out a reasonable way to convince Cat to go along, or at least not freak out about the sharp change of plans.

Tansy wasn't reassured when Cat met her at the door, eyes wild and voice shrill and too loud.

"Where the hell you *been*, Tansy? I thought the cops threw you in jail at first since you took so long, but I figured you would at least call me if that happened."

"Calm down and let me inside and I'll tell you." Tansy held up the bag. "I didn't learn near as much as I wanted to talking to anyone at the police station, so I stopped in at The Drop In and Shop to see what Mark and Tim might know. That's all."

Cat moved enough to let Tansy squeeze through before she slammed the door. Her permed hair hung in damp ringlets, and she clutched a threadbare but still fluffy in patches pink robe tight against her chest.

"That's all, huh? Nothing else I ought to know about? Then how come I just now got a call from some deputy wanting to know if you were here or not? Why'd you tell them you're *staying* here?"

"I'm not stupid, Cat." *Styu*pid. "I didn't tell them anything they didn't ask, and no one said a word about where I was staying. All I did was tell them we hung out here last night just like we worked out. Was it Deputy Salyers?"

Cat sighed hard and grabbed the bag from Tansy, jumping when the glass bottles clinked together. She peeked inside and put the whole thing down on the couch.

"I think that was her name, yeah. You think everyone knows you're here?"

Tansy shrugged and sat, being careful not to jostle the Cokes too much.

"I'd say that's a good bet, wouldn't you? Neither one of us has been trying to sneak around, and my car is parked right beside yours. You said you found me that first day because there aren't that many Georgia plates around here, remember?"

Cat curled up at the other end of the couch, feet tucked under her robe.

"Then what were they calling me for? You think they're onto us?"

"I doubt they're onto us, but they might be taking another look at me. I saw someone at The Drop In and Shop who ran with my Daddy a long time ago, and got the feeling he knew who I was. That might not have a thing to do with it, though."

"Why would he call the cops if he knew your Daddy?"

Tansy laughed, but nothing about it sounded happy.

"Because they ended up hating each other a long time before I wised up and left home. Enough so he decided he hated me and my mother too, just for fun. I think the bigger problem is this whole thing might be getting ready to blow up way outside our little corner of the coalfields. I saw Captain O'Quinn's widow at the police station. And considering how she's been spending her time over the past couple of decades, she might be bringing a big bunch of Nashville attention along with her. But I get the feeling she doesn't want all that heat any more than we do."

By the time Tansy finished with everything she'd heard and seen, Cat had one fist pushed hard against her chest. The worst part was the movement of her hand made it impossible to ignore how hard and fast she was breathing.

"If that Lee Couch guy tells them how good you are with explosives," Cat said, "*and* a crowd of cops a lot smarter than our local ones show up, we might both be done for. What are we gonna do?"

"To start with, I need you to tell me exactly what Deputy Salyers said, so we can decide what to do about that. You got any ice in the kitchen? Because I picked up our favorite after-party munchies, and I figure we could both use a little bit of comfort food and caffeine right about now. Then we'll keep on going and hope we don't crash too hard in the end."

Before they finished the junk food and a good bit more from the furnace-pantry stash—and after Cat stopped talking

—Tansy wished they had the booze or pot or anything else to go with it.

Deputy Salyers had indeed thought of a few more questions she wanted to ask. Including asking Cat where Tansy had been the night before.

Cat swearing she'd stayed with their story of getting drunk and watching bad movies only helped a little, since the deputy had still requested Tansy stop back by for a chat.

Even without anyone saying it, Tansy knew that wouldn't stay a request for long.

Their time was running out, and running off wouldn't do them any good yet.

Deputy Salyers seemed too much like the local, young cop who'd be moving up and out of Vail County before long because she was damn good at her job.

Exactly the kind of cop Tansy and Cat didn't want taking too close of a look at them. Or on their trail if they tried to disappear.

The caffeine and sugar buzz didn't magically produce any brilliant ideas of what to do next. The fried chicken with all the fixings delivery they'd ordered in from a restaurant down the street after the sweet-and-salty binge tasted better, but it didn't help much either.

"Did she sound like she'd wait until morning for me to go in?" Tansy said. "Or will that only make her more suspicious?"

Cat scrubbed her mouth with one of the thin, crinkly napkins that came with their food, shaking her head.

"She didn't exactly say, but she didn't sound too patient. She has your cell number, right? And never did call you?"

"She hasn't called yet, no. Might not be the best idea to

wait until she gets antsy enough to do that. Or she might still have her hands full with everyone else who showed up."

Tansy had another possibility floating around at the back of her mind, but she didn't dare mention it to Cat just yet. Not when she wasn't sure she'd have the guts to go through with it herself.

"I think I'm going to head back over there," Tansy said. "One of the things my Daddy said that I hated then was the longer I put something off, the worse it would get. The joke's on me now, because I always get things over with quick as I can. You gonna be okay here for a little while longer? If they haven't figured out a reason to look at you yet, probably better if you lay low so they don't come up with one."

"Don't look like I have a hell of a lot of choice. Especially since this whole crazy thing was my idea in the first place." She waved one hand at a modest flatscreen TV in the corner. "I might just watch one of those crappy movies to keep my mind off everything."

Tansy nodded and stood, then turned back to Cat.

"Listen, you ever give any thought to making a real change, Cat? Maybe getting out of here and trying somewhere new?"

Cat snorted. "And leave my little paradise here behind? 'Course I've thought about it. I just never had any idea where to go or what I'd do when I got there."

"Might be something to think more about if we get through all this, you know?"

Cat stared at Tansy, looking as surprised as Tansy felt. She hadn't exactly planned to say any of that, or to consider taking Cat with her when she left.

But the past few days had reminded her why they got along

so well in the first place. Like they softened each other's rough edges somehow, as long as they could keep from egging each other on and getting into even more trouble.

"I guess I'll think on it while you're gone," Cat finally said. "And we'll see what happens when you get back."

Tansy didn't miss the certainty that she *would* get back, one she didn't quite feel for herself.

# CHAPTER 25

THIS TIME, she had no trouble parking at the police station. All the out-of-town police SUVs were gone, and only a few other cars were scattered around the shadowy parking lot.

She hoped that meant the publicity had died down, or maybe that the cops had found some other lead to follow.

But she was afraid all the fuss and bother was only going to get worse as word got around.

A crisp chill once again pushed springtime away, and Tansy couldn't hear much besides random vehicles rolling by on the four-lane a couple of blocks away.

And the strangest aroma drifted through the air.

Sweet and kind of pungent.

Almost like someone had a way better quality weed lit than she and Cat ever managed to score, and right beside the police station of all places. Even with Virginia relaxing their tight-ass ways about marijuana, that seemed pretty damn brazen.

The flare of a lighter against a dark corner of the building warned her right before a woman spoke. Her voice was too smooth and her accent too flat to be local.

"You were here earlier."

Tansy paused, wanting to run even though this mystery person had obviously already seen her. And she couldn't see a thing with the glare of a streetlight between her and that voice.

"Yeah, a few hours ago," she said. "Mind if I ask who I'm talking to?"

A pause, the sound of inhaling, and another burst of pot smoke floated toward Tansy.

"I suppose that all depends on who's asking." The woman cleared her throat, and her words slowed and melted together a little bit, taking on the musical sound of the mountains all around them. "Since I can hear Vail County right there in your voice, ain't no point in pretending I'll ever truly be anyone in my *heart* besides Miss Lori Jane Holbrook from just down the road in Estonoa."

Low, bitter-edged laughter drifted out with the smoke, and the accent disappeared.

"But people back here can't seem to remember I was ever anyone besides the former Mrs. Captain O'Quinn. It's no better in Nashville, but they only ever knew me as that bitch who controls the music everyone wants to get their hands on. I expected better here for some crazy reason. Ever feel that way? Like you tried so hard to go home but your own people keep saying you never really belonged there in the first place?"

Tansy tried not to panic, since she'd been thinking about trying to talk to Mrs. O'Quinn—Lori Jane—for the last hour or so.

She'd either stumbled into a chance conversation that would throw the net over her at last, or a possible way out.

"I haven't quite felt that way, no," Tansy said. "Maybe because I took off the first chance I got and haven't hardly been back since. Glad to meet you, Lori Jane. I'm Tansy."

"Glad to meet you, Tansy. Want a hit?"

Tansy walked toward the voice and the scent, not sure what she was getting herself into now, but unable to resist.

"Sure. They don't mind you smoking right outside the police station?"

"Not as long as I keep cooperating, I suppose. What I think is they don't want this one to go down as a failure for Craigen and the fancy new museum. And they're convinced the best shot of flushing out whoever did this and getting the stuff back is me hanging around."

Tansy stopped just inside the line of shadow, letting her eyes adjust. The lighter flare let her know where to look as the outline of a darker figure leaning against the wall took shape.

"Just hanging around? That's all they want?"

Lori Jane handed a palm-sized glass pipe with a tiny water reservoir over, orange embers still glowing in the bowl. Tansy took a solid hit and held her breath, hoping she wouldn't cough and rip the slash on her side open again. Cooled after bubbling through water, the smoke was as smooth and sweet as it smelled.

"If I'm in town playing up the heartbroken widow angle, that brings all *kinds* of attention to this case, see? And more attention is sure to help them figure out who took off with the good stuff. The one who's still out there walking around, anyway, instead of in the chiller over at the funeral home. Not only does the museum get their prize memorabilia back, but our dear friends inside get a massive boost for cracking the case."

"I'm sorry for saying so, but you don't exactly sound thrilled about any of that."

Lori Jane shook her head and took the pipe back.

"Don't get me wrong. I want everything returned more than anyone else, even the police. I'll tell you the truth, Tansy. The only reason I donated so much of it was because seeing it around the house had a way of ripping my heart out again every single day. I figured this way the Captain O'Quinn and the Confederates legend would live on for another generation or two. That would have made Jimmy happy."

Tansy bit her lip, not wanting to blurt out that she'd had no idea Captain O'Quinn's name was Jimmy.

Not when Lori Jane sounded like he'd passed away that morning instead of years ago.

Coming back here might have made it feel exactly like that for her.

Especially when two dumbasses bought in to the redneck gossip around town saying the Widow O'Quinn didn't care about any of that stuff, or him. Then got it into their thick heads that stealing a bunch of old stuff wouldn't hurt anyone.

"I'm real sorry you had to come back here for that kind of thing, Lori Jane."

"I appreciate that, especially you remembering my name for more than a second or two. Another hit?" She waited for Tansy to shake her head. "If you don't mind me asking, what part do you play in all this? I'm guessing you didn't volunteer to answer a bunch of nosy questions twice just for the fun of it."

Just like when she was talking to Deputy Salyers, Tansy decided to get as close to the truth as she could manage. She waited for the lighter flame to reignite the fragrant dope packed into the bowl, and for Lori Jane to get her own hit and hold it for a good long while.

"No, I didn't volunteer. The one they found in the coal mine? That was my cousin."

Lori Jane let out a pot-scented cloud in a rush.

"Damn, I'm sorry about that body-over-in-the-chiller thing I said. I had no idea."

"No way you *could* know. Like I said, I've lived away for a long time, and we weren't exactly close." Tansy hesitated, then took a deep breath and forged ahead with the whisper of an idea she'd had before. "I get the feeling they think I might know who she was working with. Or where she might have stashed the stuff."

Lori Jane turned sideways toward Tansy, one shoulder against the building.

"Is that right? Now where do you think they might have gotten that idea, with you and your cousin not being close and all?"

Tansy shrugged, and took the offered pipe again. She barely dragged enough to taste it.

"They might be hoping I remember some kind of secret childhood hangout or clubhouse or something like that, not that we ever had a clubhouse. Maybe somewhere else that meant something to Vickie. Anyway, I think they hope one of the ones I do remember turns out to be the right place. I know my family hopes I can come up with something, or somebody can. They feel pretty much the same way you do about so much attention coming down the pike and aimed directly at them."

"So you don't think whoever got away and...left your cousin there, took things with them after all? You think it might be somewhere else?"

Tansy passed the pipe back.

"I wouldn't want to guess what they think, or what my cousin actually did. She had a lot of trouble in her life that finally caught up with her. About to come crashing down on my family, too. Most of them don't even deserve it. But I have a couple of places in mind they might want to check out. Maybe a way to save all of us a whole bunch of time and trouble."

Lori Jane nodded as she stared out toward the street.

"I doubt anyone at all would mind if things got put right and this whole situation faded into the past. I sure as hell wouldn't. I wonder if we might have a few things we should talk about, Tansy. That is if you're comfortable talking to me before the police. Or maybe even instead of them."

Tansy looked across the street herself, where cars had been lined up with barely room enough to walk between them only a few hours ago. And that was before word about the missing Captain O'Quinn memorabilia really got out.

Or word of Lori Jane being in town.

With Deputy Salyers ready to ask questions Tansy had no interest in answering, it was time to take a chance.

"I realize I only met you a few minutes ago," she said, "but it does seem to me we have what you might call a similar point of view on wanting this situation to clear up the easiest way it can. I'm willing to do whatever I can to help make that happen."

She heard Lori Jane breathe slow and deep, without the lighter flare or a stronger aroma of weed this time.

"Okay then. Here's what I think we should do. You go check out the areas where you think the stuff might be. Especially the gold record. That was Jimmy's pride and joy more than almost anything else. And as soon as you know one way or the other, call me from a number that won't connect you and me. A store, or restaurant, or hell, a payphone if you can dig one of those up. With me so far?"

"So far."

"Good. Then I report it as an anonymous tip. Say it must have come from some high school friend of mine from the old days, or whatever it seems like they'll believe. Once the stuff is back at the museum where it belongs, I can call this whole thing off and get the hell out of town. And you ought to strongly consider doing the same. I can promise you'll have whatever you need to do just that and not worry about money for a good long time. My insurance and the museum's will be delighted they don't have to pay out a penny. Then as long as this stays between us, everybody's happy."

Tansy closed her eyes, hearing her Auntie Louise's voice, how heartbroken and *defeated* she sounded over Vickie. And remembering how horrified she'd been herself when she realized which way the gun was pointing when it went off.

She doubted she'd ever forget the unmistakably dead weight on her own body no matter how much time passed. A nightmare had already found her even with her exhaustion, and she knew her own mind well enough to expect a boatload more where that came from.

So maybe not everyone would be what you might call *happy*.

But Tansy was old enough to understand that sometimes in life, you had to do whatever let you keep going the next day. And try your level best to do better the day after that.

"You're still making sense as far as I'm concerned," she said. "But what do we do if it turns out I can't find the stuff?"

Tansy caught a pale flash of movement around where Lori Jane's smile should be.

"You're right about us barely meeting, Tansy. But I think we understand each other well enough to know it will work out *so* much better for both of us if your hunch about that secret hiding place turns out to be true."

She pulled something out of her pants pocket and handed it to Tansy. It felt like a regular business card.

"My personal cell. Call or text me anytime, if you've got something worth telling me.

"Can I ask you one more question? Or will that blow this whole thing up in my face?"

Lori Jane was silent and unmoving for so long that Tansy worried it was already too late.

Then that lighter flare, and a long, bubbling drag.

Silence again.

And a burst of pot smoke that seemed big and strong enough to fill the whole street.

"You've got one more. Make it a good one, and take care you don't stomp on my toes too hard."

Several questions circling around in Tansy's mind demanding attention threatened to push all the words she'd ever learned right out of her head. But she managed to grab hold to what she hoped was the right one.

"Why are you trusting me with all of this? I can think of a dozen reasons why you wouldn't, but not one why you would."

A surprisingly deep laugh came out of the shadows.

"After spending my whole adult life as a woman in the cutthroat music business, I guess I learned how to make that decision pretty quick. Even if a negotiation takes weeks or longer, the truth is I know when I walk into the room, the second I'm right in front of the person, whether we're going to do business or not. I made mistakes in the beginning, no denying that. Plenty of people thought they'd have an easy time taking advantage of the poor, grieving widow, and some of them did. I learned from every single one of them. So now, most of the time, I walk away with exactly what I want."

Tansy heard water drain out of the pipe, then a small zipper closing before Lori Jane went on.

"That, and I doubt you would have said one word to me if you didn't have something to offer that would help both of us. Not once you realized who I was. We both want this unfortunate situation to dry up and go away, right? I think we both know working together is the only way to make that happen. That answer your question?"

Tansy scrubbed her face with both hands, wishing she had more time to think about it and even more of that pot to give her even a passing chance at focusing enough to figure it out.

"That answers it well enough. Thank you."

"You're welcome, Tansy. I'd just as soon keep all of this out of the local gossip mill, certainly when it comes to any compensation that might change hands. The last thing I want is a bunch of small-time petty thieves deciding they can cash out. Here and everywhere else people try to do a decent thing like setting up a museum to remember the *good* things instead of the bad. This is a one-time, only-time arrangement. Now, are you going to be the first person in a long time I regret trusting?"

"I'll do my damndest to make sure that doesn't happen, Lori Jane."

Lori Jane held out her hand—another pale blur in the shadows—and Tansy shook it. Her fingers were soft and warm, and her grip much stronger than it had any right to be.

"I hope that's true. And I hope the whole thing turns out to be worth it to both of us in the end. If you decide to talk to Deputy Salyers tonight, I'd strongly suggest doing everything you can to stall her until we make the arrangements between ourselves. She's a damn shrewd one. She also let slip that she's leaving for the night in about an hour. Not sure she *meant* for me to catch that, but one of the many things I learned from living with a songwriter is anything I overhear is fair game. Call me, anytime day or night."

She stepped out into the light and walked away from the police station. Her hair gleamed blonde and flashed silver under the streetlights, and she didn't so much as glance back.

Tansy stood still for a few seconds, not sure whether she'd just got hold of a lifeline or the exact amount of rope she needed to hang herself and Cat at the same time.

One thing she did know was she had no business speaking to Deputy Salyers or anyone else who carried a badge and gun.

Not until she got her head clear and talked to Cat.

And she got a second opinion about her idea of a believable place to stash their unsellable pile of Captain O'Quinn memorabilia long enough to send it right back where it came from.

# CHAPTER 26

TANSY WATCHED Cat pacing an obviously a well-worn worry path around her tiny apartment.

From the front door, where she touched the scuffed fake-gold doorknob, to the window, where she twitched the flimsy curtain aside to reveal the night, then back into place. A loop by the brick-hard couch for a brush at invisible wrinkles in the sheets Tansy had folded along the back, then a pause to glare at the dark flatscreen TV, as if it would sprout fur, ears, and a tail if Cat didn't watch it often enough.

An occasional pass through the petite but pin-neat kitchen, where Tansy imagined Cat running a dishtowel over the warped baby-blue laminate counter and across a dented but functional bright-yellow electric stove. Maybe peeked into her cramped pantry closet with shelves jammed in around the useless furnace to check her supplies of beer, soda, chips, and all kinds of cheap quick-cooking options.

While Cat paced off her anxiety and threatened to wear a path in thin brown carpet that almost gave enough padding to disguise the concrete slab underneath, Tansy sat curled up in the armchair and waited.

Too keyed up about the escape hatch Lori Jane O'Quinn had (maybe) dropped into her lap to relax, and too tired to get up and do something useful.

Though getting into Cat's path while she was deep in thought probably wasn't the best idea in the world, even compared to how their other brilliant ideas had gone over the last couple of days.

When Cat wasn't fussing with straightening up messes only she could see, she ran her fingertips along the too-long ties of her ratty pink robe, or fluffed up her already towering perm-curls, or rubbed her knuckles over and over again. She never cracked her knuckles like Tansy too often did, but the repetitive motion was plenty annoying without the noise.

But Tansy refused to say a word. Especially through the sweet, floaty euphoria Lori Jane's pot had set loose in her brain. She didn't think it would last all that long, thank goodness. But she wouldn't turn down more if she got the chance.

But not tonight. One reason Tansy rarely smoked was she was usually ready for her head to clear a lot sooner than the marijuana was ready to give up its influence.

And she needed her head as clear as it could be right now.

After all, it wasn't every day someone got asked to make the kind of choice Cat was wrestling with right now.

Never mind that the two of them hadn't had anywhere near that much trouble deciding to blast a hole under the museum so they could make off with a bunch of supposedly useless junk to scrounge up easy money.

That basic idea had turned out to be so pitiful—and dangerous—that Tansy couldn't even laugh about how horribly wrong they'd been.

"I just don't *know*, Tansy." Cat stopped in front of the couch and crossed her arms, staring at the ceiling. "She might be working with the cops, trying to trick us into giving ourselves up. What if they got somebody watching for us to go somewhere and they follow us?"

"I can't promise you a thing, you know that. Except now I'm not the only one who sees how Deputy Salyers has a fire in her belly about getting this case solved. It already wasn't going to look great for the museum or the town at all if the Captain O'Quinn stuff disappeared into thin air, but I was foolish enough to figure they'd get over it eventually. Or give up and stop looking. But with what sure does look like a murderer on the loose thrown into the mix, they're in overdrive trying to figure it out."

Cat shook her head slowly as she sank onto the couch.

"I'm not saying I want us to test it out, mind you, but I really think that would go as self-defense, don't you? Vickie did hide and wait for us, and she had a knife, remember?"

The calm Tansy had been working so hard to build up like a shell around the fact that she'd killed a person—accident or not—cracked and sizzled away between one breath and the next. That or the tension in her whole body set the cut to throbbing again.

Her voice came out tight and mean, as if that breath had scorched her throat on the way in.

"You keep *saying* that, Cat, and I'm gonna tell you this one more time that it doesn't *matter*. No, I didn't aim my gun and fire on purpose, but it *was* my gun. She still ended up dead with her blood all over me. And do you really expect me to waltz into the police station and try to convince them that we just happened to be out there but we weren't involved with stealing from the museum? No chance in hell that flies, but I guess that's easy enough for you to say since you wouldn't be facing down the difference between robbery and murder."

Cat blinked and drew her knees up to her chest, pulling the ridiculous robe tight around her knees. Her scowl wasn't any less angry for including a deeply bruised and swollen eye.

"I wasn't *trying* to make it sound like I'd do that," she said, "trying to cut you loose and push the blame your way. I know we might not get out of this no matter how hard we twist and squirm. But I don't think it helps anyone to *expect* things to get worse than they already are. Except maybe the cops. Unless that's who you want to help, since *you* got someplace to go if you decide to run."

Tansy covered her eyes with one hand and counted to five inside her mind.

As well as she got along with Cat and always had, they had two rotten ways of tuning each other up. Talking each other into doing something *styu*pid, and getting angry in a flash when that could only cause the situation to get worse.

"I'm not trying to help the cops, Cat. I doubt either one of us saw all of this coming, I know I didn't. But they might not need anyone's help. We *both* rushed into a job that would have been tricky to pull off no matter what, even before Vickie showed up. All I'm trying to do is find us a way out of this that doesn't mean looking over our shoulders for the rest of our lives."

Cat's scowl deepened, and her red cheeks had Tansy worried she'd only keep getting madder. But she slowly relaxed, and even smiled a tiny bit.

"We probably did charge in too fast, can't argue with that one. But up until Vickie showed up, we did pull it off. Beat to shit and more than half done in, sure. We *did* do it."

Tansy shook her head, trying to resist the shifting mood despite not wanting to get into an argument. Then whatever prideful part of her thinking came straight from her Daddy took over and she smiled.

"Yeah, we did, didn't we? And not one part of it was easy. So let's see if we can't get through this next part with our hides in one piece. I got an idea of where we might hide the stuff, and most folks in town know how bad Vickie was obsessed with the place. Do you know if anyone ever bought that old—"

Both of them jumped at a sharp knock at the front door.

"You normally get folks dropping by after ten o'clock?" Tansy knew in her gut that didn't matter, but she was grasping for any other answer than what she suspected.

Cat shook her head slowly as her face went from flushed to pale.

"Not hardly ever. Pretty much anyone who drops by calls first anyway. You think that deputy decided to come here instead of going home after all?"

Tansy got to her feet, wishing her hands hadn't started shaking and sweating at the same time.

"Wish I could say no. No point in pretending we're not

here with the cars out there and lights on. Any point in trying to cover up those bruises on your face?"

Cat touched the purple puffiness around her eye, then moved down to the much less noticeable swelling around her lips.

"I never did much wear makeup, you know that. Doubt I have anything that would work even if most of it wasn't at least five years old. Maybe we got so drunk watching our movies that I tripped and fell?"

The knock repeated, louder than before. Tansy hadn't realized how impatient—and threatening—someone's fist hitting a thin wooden door could sound.

"That'll have to do. I guess you should answer since you live here, huh?"

Cat jumped up and fussed with her hair again, then re-tied her robe into a sad, droopy bow.

"I look disreputable enough to bust my head in my own living room, don't I? Might as well get on with it."

In the few seconds it took for Cat to cross the little room and reach for the doorknob, Tansy's mind seized up panic-solid.

Screaming at her that Cat had just mentioned the blasted knife, the one Vickie used to try to slice Tansy into two pieces.

The knife that had more of Tansy's blood all over it than Vickie's.

She had no idea whether it was still out at the pot mine, somewhere in Cat's apartment with Tansy's own gun, or already on the way to the crime labs in Richmond or wherever Virginia cops sent evidence in a high-profile murder case.

And the deputy Lori Jane rightly called damn shrewd had to be the one Cat was about to let in the door.

Her arms and legs froze as hard as her throat when a deep, gravely voice yelled from the other side of the door.

"I know you're in there, Tansy Marie. I don't guess you want to make this worse on you than it already is."

# CHAPTER 27

CAT YANKED her hand back and clutched it to her chest, looking for all the world like she'd scorched it on a hot cooktop, and whirled to face Tansy.

Tansy did her best not to slump back down into the chair, torn between feeling too weary to deal with one more damn thing and spitting furious about getting dragged back into her family's past on top of everything else.

"Aw hell, I'll get it. This one's all about me. Unless he's changed more than anything else around here, he'll stay out there and pound on your door until the sun comes up. No need for you to deal with this particular asshole."

Cat stepped back but stayed close by, and Tansy was glad for the backup. Whatever good it might do.

Then Tansy opened the door for exactly the scruffy old man she expected. He'd blend in just fine anywhere in Craigen and Vail County like he had at the Drop In and Shop, dressed in the typical local redneck uniform of ancient blue jeans, a faded blue t-shirt with the neck stretched out, a grubby brown Carhartt jacket, and gray work boots that had to be at least thirty years old. Even the mixed smells of coffee, cigarette smoke, and old sweat fit right in.

But this particular redneck stood out to her and always would.

Her Daddy's best-friend-turned-worst-enemy.

Lee Couch.

Still wearing that ugly orange UT cap and staring down his bumpy nose at her, but not scowling this time. When he pulled the cap off and revealed a head still full of the stringy white hair she remembered from a long time ago—but now with a hat-shaped circle pressed against his head—Tansy was surprised at having to choke back a laugh.

Lee clearly misunderstood that choke for fear instead of amusement.

Because now his dark blue eyes twinkled, and his expression ran a lot closer to the shit-eating smirk she could have gone the rest of her life without ever seeing again.

"Can't exactly say I'm glad to see you here, Lee, but I'll admit I'm surprised. Guess you forgot your business with me and my family came to an end the day we put my Daddy in the ground."

Lee grinned and laughed like the sound gravels made under a truck's tires. The unmistakable stink of whiskey rolled out with the laugh, a change from his ever-present beer sweat Tansy remembered too well.

"Now that's no way to say howdy to me after all these many long years, little girl. Why should all that nasty business between me and Virge keep me and you from a pleasant reunion this fine evening?"

He moved to step inside, but Tansy shifted into the middle of the doorway. She was happy to give way when Cat stood firm by her shoulder.

"That's about all the reunion I've got the stomach for," Tansy said. "So you best be on your way and find someone else to bother."

Lee's tremendous frown might have made a stranger think he was heartbroken at being rejected. Only if they didn't notice the delighted crinkles around his eyes.

"Now ain't that rich. I make a special trip just to see you after all this time, and you don't so much as invite me inside for a chat. Seems like you forgot all the manners your folks worked so hard to teach you."

Tansy snorted. "My manners are just fine, such as they ever were. What I didn't forget is how you treated my Daddy and all the rest of us after you two had your falling out. As far as my Momma, she never much cared for you in the first place. I think she was happy when you finally stopped dragging yourself over to our house. Anyway, so sorry you went to all the trouble, Lee, but we got better things to do."

She went to close the door, but Lee shoved his heavy foot against it.

"You might *think* you got better things to do, Tansy Marie. But I gar-un-*tee* you'll wish you hadn't been such a snotty-ass brat to me before the sun comes up."

Tansy crossed her arms but didn't move. She was angrier at having one more damn thing to deal with than she was afraid of Lee's threats. So far.

"You don't say? So at least one more thing that never changes around here is how much you love the sound of your own mouth running. Never much mattered to you if everyone else kept handing you another beer, hoping and praying you'd pass out or find someone else to yak at. Any chance you'll get the hell out of here and leave me alone if you get to sing your little song?"

"I reckon you'll change your own tune before I'm done. You gonna make me stand here like some kind of stranger instead of inviting me in?"

"What I *want* to do is slam the door on your foot hard enough that you'll have a hell of a time working the gas pedal on your way out to your house, or wherever you fetch up for the night these days. But it's not my place, so not my say."

Tansy waved one hand toward Cat.

"Seems to me Tansy's made herself mighty clear," Cat said. "And I might have heard plenty about you over the years, but you're nothing but a stranger to me. Can't say I feel sorry about that, either. So if you're determined to say your piece, you just stand right there and say it."

This time Lee's squinty eyes and scowl were real, and he jammed his fists onto his hips like Tansy'd seen him do hundreds of times a long time ago.

"If that's the way you feel about it, I might as well go on home and leave your ass to twist in the wind."

"Good." Tansy reached for the doorknob to shove the door closed, wishing it would be as easy as that. The other thing Lee Couch couldn't seem to do without was a good, long buildup of drama when he had something to say.

Especially if he knew it would cause trouble for someone else and couldn't wait to tell them so.

"Yeah, you're Virge Stidham's little girl through and through, ain't you? Enough so I won't be the only one to put together your little trip to the farm supply with a neat little hole blowed right through the floor of that new museum in town."

Tansy rolled her eyes, pretending he'd just said the most ridiculous thing she'd ever heard in her life. Mainly hoping he'd believe that instead of guessing how her gut twisted and rolled at his words.

Thank goodness Cat picked up on the game right away instead of letting her own feelings show.

"Lord, he does love to run his mouth, don't he? Almost as much as he loves his whiskey from the smell of him. What in the hell are you carrying on about now?"

"I'm carrying on about one too many things that fit together for the cops to ignore," Lee said, "even the local dipshits. Tansy here shows up after years away. Then a bunch of crap goes missing from the museum and her cousin Vickie shows up dead. Mind you I'm not *about* to pretend that real sweetheart of a girl didn't spend a lifetime making every enemy she could, so that one's not exactly a surprise."

Lee kept one hand on his hip and pointed at Tansy with the other.

"But then I hear tell of a blast so clean it could of been a hot knife through butter? And little Tansy Marie just happens to be in town, and happens to go out to the farm supply and set Vickie into some kind of tizzy? And all these years I thought *I* was the only one ever came close to being as good with blowing things up as Virge Stidham was."

He swung his gnarled and rude forefinger over to Cat.

"Now this part I admit I didn't put together until I heard where she's been crashing. Because I sure as shit remember Cat Maybell's kinfolks being neck-deep in that dope mine nonsense way back when. And here the two of you are, cozy as two kittens in a sunbeam."

Tansy laughed, hoping it sounded amused or disgusted instead of scared half out of her mind.

"Sounds to me like you're almost as good at spinning a great big pile of horseshit as Vickie was. Not one word of that makes sense. And even if it did, you expect us to believe you have some kind of inside line on this whole investigation? What, you drinking buddies with the cops now?"

Lee put his hand back on his hip and stared up at the ceiling, as if the popcorn surface or one of Cat's upstairs neighbors might be able to give him patience.

"That's the thing everyone running around with their noses glued to those damn phones never did understand. I don't need no inside line or search engine or reality television, or whatever else folks decide gives them the truth. I know how to listen, and who to listen to. *I* just happen to know one of the boys who did the renovation work on that old Vance place before the museum moved in. Turns out he got called in to look at the damage this morning. Easy as birthday cake to get him talking."

Tansy could practically feel Cat's worry and tension piling up, probably about as much as her own was. That had to be what the Grouchy Old Men's Hot Dog Committee meeting was about that afternoon at the Drop In and Shop.

Before she could coax anything sensible out of her own mouth, Cat jumped in.

"And *that's* what made you think of Tansy and me? Gonna have to do a whole lot better than that to get whatever the hell you want from us. Not that you said a word about that yet. I don't much believe you stopped by out of the goodness of your heart."

Lee slipped his hands into his pockets and leaned forward.

"Well, let's just say I also got wind there's about to be a nice, juicy reward on the table for whoever gets the stuff returned. And since I came by here instead of going straight to the cops, I reckon it would be real nice of you to share a good bit of that with me."

Tansy shook her head and smiled.

"You think we'll turn in the junk you're so convinced we stole, *and* that we'll get a reward for the whole mess? Why the hell would the cops do that? Then you think we'll agree to turn around and give you some of it? I believe all these years have run you more than half crazy."

"No ma'am, I don't expect that, because I know better than to trust you or any other Stidham. What I expect is you'll show me where the stuff is hidden right there behind you. Or *tell* me where the stuff is somewhere else, and maybe we'll go out there together. Then I listen in when you make your I'm-such-a-very-good-little-girl phone call to the police. All you got to do then is hand over the cash when the time comes, because you know exactly what *I'll* do if you try to make a run for it first."

# CHAPTER 28

TANSY STARED at her Daddy's one-time best friend, having to force herself not to shake her head. She'd thought Lee was kind of an annoying nitwit back then, but like her Mama, she put up with him because of the friendship.

Now she realized she was looking at a pure old Vail County dumbass who'd somehow managed to keep himself going for every bit of seventy years or more.

He honestly expected her and Cat to turn over the stolen memorabilia, or lead him right to it, and trust him not to either crack their skulls or turn them in right then or later on. Once that was done, of course he'd have to trust *them* to pay up.

His big plan didn't make a damn bit of sense. But he didn't seem to realize that.

The longer it stayed that way, the better.

"I got no problem with all the cops in the county waltzing in to search," Cat said, "because there ain't a thing here for them to find. No idea where you get your red-hot ideas from, but you made a wrong turn a long ways back with this one."

Lee nodded, swallowing Cat's bait in one gulp.

"Now that one I believe. Ain't a thing *here* to find. Already got it tucked away somewhere else, I'd say. Keep running your mouths, both of you. The more you fuss and carry on, the more you prove my damn point. I'll give you one last chance to get your heads out of your asses before I bust inside and get the job done. If that don't work, I got a bunch of rowdy boys who'd be more than happy to help."

"Don't guess you'd be willing to give us a couple of minutes to think it over," Tansy said. "You know, maybe even talk it over between ourselves."

Again that gravely laugh.

"Why sure, *'course* I would. Least I can do for Virge's little girl. Since you both made it clear I'm not welcome to set foot inside Cat's grand palace here, you can just step right out into the parking lot. I'll take myself far enough away that I won't be tempted to listen in, once I know for sure you don't have a gun or a knife or one of those goddamned cell phones in your pockets."

The mention of a knife started an idea going in Tansy's mind. But she wasn't about to stand there long enough to let Lee see it taking shape on her face. She patted down her pockets, pulling out her car keys, phone, wallet, and Lori Jane's plain white business card, then walked back to drop them on Cat's coffee table.

She did make sure the card landed upside down.

Cat didn't even look Tansy's way. She just pulled a tube of lip balm out of one of her robe's pockets and her huge phone out of the other, and turned both pockets inside out to show they were otherwise empty. She grabbed her own keys from the same coffee table.

"I imagine you won't mind if I lock up behind myself," she said, jingling them at Lee. "Landlord says we all got to watch out for suspicious characters trying to sneak inside."

Lee snorted and took a few steps backward and away from the door.

"Whatever floats your damn boat down the bullshit river. Just get out here so we can get this over with."

A typical overly huge modern pickup truck with its big engine still ticking to itself dwarfed Cat's sedan. Despite the rest of the automotive world leaving the problems of rust behind decades ago, Tansy recognized the dark pattern of metallic rot against the light paint over the shiny bald tires and along the crusty running boards.

Lee walked around and leaned against the tailgate, waving one hand toward the empty space beyond before he energetically crossed his arms.

Cat grabbed Tansy's arm too hard as they walked toward the sidewalk, under bright orange streetlights that would be mobbed by about ten thousand bugs once summer really settled in. The spring night had rolled in too cool for anything like that.

They faced away from Lee and leaned their heads together.

"I hope you got something in mind so we can get him the hell out of here, Tansy. He's too damn squirrely for me, and now he knows where I *live*."

Tansy patted Cat's hand so she'd finally let go of her pinching grip.

"I got an idea of where to send him, sure, if it's as empty as the last time I was out there. Might solve two problems for us before the night's through. Did anyone ever buy the old Harbury place?"

Cat drew back and blinked, her skin showing pumpkin-colored in the light.

"The one with the barn bigger than the house, and a bunch of overgrown apple trees behind it? Last I know, nothing but a bunch of feral cats and possums live out there." She scowled. "That the same one you said Vickie accused someone of buying to keep her from it?"

"The very same. I was thinking earlier that would be a good place for us to dump the stuff, then tell Lori Jane so she can tip the cops. A whole lot of folks around here know how Vickie carried on about that house. Could have been her stashing it there, or whoever took her out. Either way, it's believable enough to work."

"None of it's out there yet, though, and Lee's breathing down our necks right now. How we gonna..." Cat covered her mouth with one hand, eyes wide. "You ain't saying we dump *him* out there, are you?"

Tansy took a deep breath, then glanced over her shoulder to make sure Lee was still sulking by his truck.

"I never did like him, not even when he and my Daddy were such good friends. And right now he's pretty damn sure he's got us beat. Makes me purely sick to say it, but he might be right about that. Unless we're both willing to try to outrun him tonight and never look back, I don't know what else we can do."

Even though most of Tansy's mind was busy skittering

around and looking for a way out, any way out, part of her whispered this wasn't a line she wanted to cross. Not on purpose.

What happened out at the mine had been more than bad enough, even considering Cat's insistence the whole thing had been self-defense.

But this wasn't even in the same neighborhood.

Luring someone out there, *meaning* to murder him with the same gun.

Taking an action to end another human being's life.

Tansy wasn't sure how Vickie's death was going to affect her as the days, weeks, and hopefully years passed.

*Planning* to kill even an asshole like Lee couldn't help but turn out a thousand times worse.

Cat didn't seem any more comfortable with the idea when she wrapped her arms around herself.

"Hell, I don't know, Tansy. You really think you could *do* that?"

Tansy shrugged. "Maybe, but I'm not sure if either one of us *should*. You got any other ideas?"

Cat slowly shook her head, but her eyes were too intent and focused for Tansy to believe the wheels inside her head weren't driving about as fast as Cat did behind the wheel.

Lee cleared his throat in what he surely thought was an intimidating way. Tansy only held up one hand, her fingers curled so only her index finger showed.

Not the finger she felt like using, but close enough.

"I feel just the same way you do about not wanting to go through all this trouble and fuss and end up with nothing," she said. "But maybe we could just...you know...*give* him the stuff.

Make it his problem instead of ours. Doubt he could sell any of it any more than we could."

Tansy pulled her lips inside against her teeth again without thinking, then realized how raw and sore they were already getting.

"I doubt he could too. But I doubt even more he's figured that out. All he's thought about so far is getting the reward money."

"Which he could do, I guess," Cat said. "If he can get to the cops before we turn him in."

"No, hang on. We don't even have to do that, remember? All I have to do is call or text Lori Jane and she'll take care of that part for us. Shit, I'll even give Lee a great insider tip on where to store the stuff so they can grab him there."

Cat stared at Tansy, finally looking excited instead of scared.

"I say we give him what we've got *and* tell him the rest is already out there. Maybe even tell him we grabbed some of that Nashville crap after all."

"I don't think we'll have to hand over everything, and I promise he'll still fall for it. Even if we give him all of it but that triple-damned gold record that got us started into all this craziness, that would send him out there right quick. And we'd get Lori Jane even more on our side by keeping it out of his nasty hands in the first place."

"How much do you trust him, Tansy? Is he gonna try to hurt us? Like *really* hurt us?"

Tansy held her breath for a few seconds before letting it out in a rush.

"I don't trust him worth a damn under any circumstances.

But with all the carousing he and my Daddy got up to—and everything I heard about him after they had their falling out— he never did actually hurt anyone. Not physically, anyway. He's not much more than your average garden-variety bully, which he proved more times than I like to think about to me and my Mom after Daddy passed."

Tansy stopped and shook her head, ignoring a strong desire to spit after her words brought those unpleasant memories back to sickening life in her mind.

"Likes to talk big standing behind someone bigger," she went on, "and especially about someone who's not there. And even more when it comes to women. His kind of backstabbing doesn't draw blood. Not unless someone socks him in the nose for it, which hasn't happened near often enough if you ask me."

Cat giggled, back to her little girl version.

"All you got to do is look at him to see how many times that's happened. I figure a guy like that could always use a few more good smacks. Think one of us is gonna have to go out there with him? I hate to think of anyone in that truck with him the way he stinks of drinking."

"Better if we don't. If one of us has to, the other can get word to Lori Jane right quick. I'll show you the card when we go back inside. Know what he said about thinking he was the only one as good as my Daddy with explosives? From what I remember and what Daddy told me, that was all inside Lee's mind. But he's a lot like Vickie was, because he told that to everyone under the sun. Anyway, unless he found himself a brand-new brain somewhere, he's the kind to reel himself in once we get him on the hook."

Lee yelled then, more than loud enough to wake the neighbors.

"You two done run your mouths about long enough! I got things to do!"

The very best thing he could do to keep Tansy's plan rolling along

Cat and Tansy smiled at each other before turning and strolling his way.

"Just keep yourself settled down, Lee," Tansy said, pushing down with both of her hands like she was trying to keep an overeager pup from jumping on her legs. "You want to rouse the whole town and county so they'll know all about this little operation?"

He shoved away from his rusty truck but didn't move toward her.

"There might be things I care about less in the world than agitating one of the lazy saps who live around here, but damned if I can think of one right now. Doubt a single person in this building has a job to get to in the morning. You two ladies come to your senses? Or do we start this thing off in a bad way?"

"I don't know if there's one sensible thing about any of this," Tansy said, glancing at Cat. "But the best we can aim for might be to get you out of our hair. Trouble is not everything you're looking for is easy to get hold of. Might have to take a little trip to get some of it."

Lee snorted and shook his head, but he did lower his voice.

"And you figure I'll play along with *that* load of crap? Why in the hell would someone move stuff that's worth a damn around like that?"

"*Because* it's worth a damn," Cat said. "I'd say you showing up and pounding my door down and standing out here yelling in the parking lot proves us right."

Tansy waved her arm toward the police station.

"That, and word is the cop they've got on the case is better than most of the locals. I've been dodging another interview all day long. That one might show up any minute now, and then we'll *all* get hauled in."

Lee narrowed his eyes and turned toward the empty street as if Deputy Salyers and the small cop army Tansy had seen at the police station might appear out of the chilly night air.

"So you're saying you give me what's easy to get to," he said, "then we all load up for a field trip and drive out of here all sweet and innocent? Know where they got a stakeout set up, do you?"

"Nope, not at all," Tansy said. "But I'm gonna guess the more time passes, the more likely they are to decide to come and encourage me to show up for that interview. And they might just decide to search Cat's place while they're at it."

Cat drew her robe more tightly around herself and shivered.

"Truth is I'm half-ass dressed because you interrupted us getting ready to take the rest out there. We already stashed away what you might call the best parts of the lot. Probably worth the most when it comes to the collector types with more money than sense, too. Especially the rich ones from Nashville."

# CHAPTER 29

Tansy fought back a smile when Lee's bushy eyebrows went up.

If he believed they'd grabbed any of the truly valuable stuff on loan to the museum, his insider sources weren't nearly as good as he thought. More likely they were yanking his chain on purpose. Probably trying to get him to leave them alone to do their jobs.

Spinning all kinds of fun tall tales, never imagining he'd actually try to do something about it.

Kind of like she was.

"Okay then," he said, "how do I know you're not stringing me along and wasting my time? Or trying to get me somewhere so I'll look like the guilty one when you call all the cops in the county down on my head?"

Tansy wasn't surprised Lee had at least a faint idea of what was going on, but didn't seem to know how to resist and get free of that hook settling itself into his jaw. Much less take the next step and walk away.

"Then think about this," Tansy said. "We hand over what we got here. That leaves you with the goods and us empty handed until we get out there. Won't be anything here to find if the cops do show up tonight."

A mean little smile lifted one corner of his mouth.

"Well, I reckon I could do you that favor. Keep you out of trouble you don't need." He snapped his wrinkled fingers and grinned. "I don't guess you want to go dragging all over creation this time of night. Not with an old cuss like me, anyway. How about I go get what you already got hidden away so you don't have to?"

It was everything Tansy could do not to grin right back at him.

"I ain't so sure about that," Cat said with a perfectly straight face. "How do we know you'll come back? Or give us our share of the reward money?"

"I bet Tansy still remembers where I live, don't you? It's not like anyone in Vail County couldn't track me down right quick. Surely you feel like that's enough to keep an old man honest."

Tansy doubted all the money Lori Jane had stashed away in her Nashville bank would keep him honest, with her or anyone else.

"I remember, Lee. And don't think I won't show up on your doorstep with every last inch of the Stidham temper I'm sure you haven't forgotten. But one more thing you might want to consider before you go hauling off after the treasure."

A flash of his own temper showed in his eyes, and he was leaning to the right like his truck keys were dragging him that way. That or the bottle of whatever he had stashed inside the cab.

"And what might that be, little girl?"

"I did see a whole mess of cops in town over this, from all over the county and more. A bunch of people are paying a lot of attention right now. If one of them happens to see you and gets suspicious, you'll have every last bit of the stolen stuff with you. Like you just said, anyone in the county could track you down, which means they know all the trouble you get yourself into. Why wouldn't they decide *you're* the one who did the job in the first place?"

Lee shook his head and chuckled, now sounding like gravels tumbling through a huge barrel full of motor oil.

"Let's say I got a way with the fine folks down at the police station." He pronounced it *po*-lice. "Always did. Not a thing in the world you want to trouble yourself with. All you got to do is point me in the right direction, and you two can get on back inside and snuggled down safe and sound for the night. You won't have to worry yourself about a single thing."

Tansy met Cat's gaze, once again amazed at how neither one of them burst out laughing. Tansy would have bet every last penny of the reward money she still hoped to get from Lori Jane that Lee wouldn't stand a whisper of a chance against Deputy Salyers.

Hell, she'd bet twice as much that even if he did know some of the locals in Craigen, he still had enough history of one kind or another of irritating local law enforcement to convince the cops he was behind the whole thing.

"Okay then," Tansy said. "Cat, if you want to go get the stuff, I'll tell Lee how to get out to the old Harbury place."

Lee pulled his keys out of his pocket, jingling them in the palm of his hand.

"*That's* where you got it all hid? Got to admit it makes good sense with the way that cousin of yours ran her mouth about someone keeping her from buying it. Hell, I don't guess I need directions out there. What'd you do, lug it all down to the basement? Not much else left of that place that ain't covered over with kudzu these days."

"Seemed like a good idea to us too," Cat said. "You'll find what you're looking for in the basement for sure. Just got to watch out for a regular curtain of cobwebs down there. Spiders still hiding out in some of them, too."

"That's where you'll find Captain O'Quinn and the Confederates' one and only gold record," Tansy said as Cat trotted toward her apartment. "Some of the Nashville stuff is nice and all, but we figured that was the real prize."

Lee leaned against the truck's front door, one foot up on the mud-caked running board step, keys still in hand.

"You probably figured right on that one, but you always did have a pretty good sensible way about you. About the most sense out of your whole family, truth be told."

Tansy smiled, not caring how many of her teeth showed.

"You know how it goes, Lee. I learned everything I really needed to know in life at my own Daddy's knee."

Lee raised his eyebrows again and opened his mouth, but before he had a chance to reply, and faster than Tansy could have believed, Cat opened her apartment door and peeked out.

"Ain't nobody else out here, is there?"

"Safe as it ever was," Tansy said.

Cat looked around anyway before she brought out a tattered brown cardboard moving box that jingled faintly with every step. Sure enough, the broken tambourine sat on top of all the lyrics and other odds and ends they'd grabbed.

"Most of this here stuff is signed," Cat said. "Or scribbled on, at least. They had all the little signs at the museum saying what it was, but we didn't have time to get hold of 'em."

Lee peered into the box, his lower lip poked out.

"Guess this is enough to start with. Be plenty for the cops to run you in if they caught you with it, anyway."

He walked around to the passenger side and tucked it into the messy passenger side floorboard. By the time he arranged a mess of plastic shopping bags, fast food bags, and filthy rags that would have fit right in when the old coal mine was still operating, Tansy couldn't tell the box was there at all.

But she had no doubt anyone who knew what they were looking for would be able to find it.

He took his time getting back around to the driver's side and let out a long, gusty sigh.

"I'd hate to find out you two was holding out on me. Keeping all the best of the goods here and sending me chasing around for a bunch of junk, trying to prove some kind of point about things that happened a long time ago."

Tansy shrugged and unrolled a lie that felt just fine slipping between her teeth.

"I don't guess I have any reason to hold out on you. Whatever happened between you and my Daddy was just that. Between you two. And like you said, having the real valuable things here would only be asking for trouble."

"And trouble is the *last* thing we want." Cat somehow managed to look and sound sincere. "I got to admit I didn't expect so many people to kick up a fuss over all this. Just as well you're gonna handle getting the rest."

Lee put his grimy orange UT hat back on and tapped the brim with his fingertips.

"Glad I could be of help. Don't you girls worry about a thing. I'll get you taken care of."

Tansy and Cat stood by the apartment door, watching until he got his pickup backed up and headed out, leaving a cloud reeking of burned up motor oil behind him.

"You think he'll go right out there?" Cat said.

"Probably have that truck redlined the whole way. He's enough of an arrogant asshole to believe he'll get away with everything. Listen, I'm gonna run down to the Drop In and Shop and make that call to Lori Jane before Lee decides to do something stupid."

"Like try to go down in that basement and break his fool neck? Better get to it."

Cat turned to open the door just as another vehicle rolled into the parking lot.

This time it was a police SUV.

And Tansy knew exactly who would step out before the low rumble of the engine cut off.

"You got your hiding place all closed up, right?" she whispered to Cat.

"They could send a whole troop of cops over here and I wouldn't worry one little bit." Cat touched Tansy's arm. "But you got to get in touch with Lori Jane before Lee gets out there, don't you?"

Deputy Salyers got out of the SUV, still dressed in her dark blue uniform. And frowning.

"Miss Stidham. I was hoping to see you back down at the station a while back."

Tansy walked toward her, being careful to keep her hands in plain sight. She heard Cat close the apartment door.

"I'm real sorry about that, Deputy. I guess I was a lot more tired from the other night than I thought. Tried to take a quick nap and ended up sleeping the whole day away. You had some more questions for me?"

Deputy Salyers leaned against the SUV's hood, crossing her arms kind of like Lee had. But Tansy didn't pretend for one second that she was as easy to manipulate and twist up as he'd been.

"I was more wondering if you'd remembered anything else you might want to tell me. Sometimes a little time to think things over does wonders for the memory. A nice long nap doesn't hurt, either."

Tansy shook her head, keeping her expression calm. At least she hoped so.

Inside she was watching her countdown clock shift from green to orange. It took a good while to get out to the old Harbury place, but they didn't have a whole lot of time to spare.

Not if she was going to get word to Lori Jane before it was too late.

"Not a thing comes to mind," she said. "Come on inside if you want. I doubt it would bother Cat if you want to sit down and chat for a minute."

Deputy Salyers watched Tansy for a few long, slow breaths.

"One thing I want to make sure you understand, Miss Stidham. I'm not accusing you of a thing, or Miss Maybell. Not right now. But other officers do know where I am."

Tansy held both empty hands out to the side.

"I understand exactly why you say that. Neither one of us has anything to hide. Cat would probably let you check it out for yourself first if you want."

"That won't be necessary. Neither one of you have any violent crimes, on record. And you both checked out more-or-less clear. After you."

# CHAPTER 30

Tansy started to knock first to make sure Cat knew they were on the way in, but Deputy Salyers already knew their arrangement over the past few days.

Knocking to go into an apartment she'd been crashing in was just one of the many possible dumb things that could trip her up hard enough to fall all the way to jail.

Or prison.

Cat was just stepping out of her bedroom wearing jeans and a blue t-shirt instead of the silly pink robe.

"I told Deputy Salyers you wouldn't mind if we talk in here," Tansy said. "Hope that's okay."

"I guess it'll have to be." Cat's smile lightened the words. "Nah, that's fine. Either one of you need something to drink? Wasn't expecting company besides Tansy, but I'm sure I can scare something up."

Deputy Salyers still stood inside the doorway, hands on her

wide belt, gaze moving everywhere around the cramped living room at once. No doubt taking inventory of every tiny thing.

"No thank you. I won't take up too much of your time."

Tansy and Cat sat on the scratchy brick-hard couch, while Deputy Salyers sat on the edge of the matching chair, still glancing into every crack and crevice. The urge to jump in and start asking questions prickled along the inside of Tansy's mind like an army of Georgia fire ants. But she managed to keep her mouth shut.

"You might already know we've completed our search of your cousin's apartment," Deputy Salyers said. "A few things are still under investigation, but I'm confident Miss Stidham never had any of the missing items from the museum there. Not that she'd have a lot of room to keep anything out of sight."

Tansy remembered her Auntie Louise calling Vickie's rental of a single room in a building full of them highway robbery, but decided now wasn't the time to mention anything like that. All she did was nod.

"I never was there for myself, but I hear those places are pretty small."

Deputy Salyers shrugged. "Quick and easy enough to search. Anyway, the reason I'm here is less about your cousin and more about what happened at the museum. Word around town is you're pretty good with explosives."

Tansy chewed the insides of her cheeks to keep from swearing. The only person who could have put that particular bug into the deputy's ear was currently on his way out to the old Harbury place.

With a box full of extremely incriminating evidence in his rusty damn truck.

"I learned a bit from my father, sure. I don't think he ever explained much of what he knew how about blowing things up to anyone else besides an old friend of his. Named Lee Crouch or Coach, something like that. I worked a few crews doing road work and structure demolition over the years, but not much more than that. Not sure why you'd ask about that now."

Deputy Salyers narrowed her eyes at Lee's name, but didn't show any other reaction.

"It is a bit of an unusual skill. Requires unusual supplies most people don't see every day. More than you might be able to find at a typical small-town farm supply, for example."

"I suppose so." Tansy thanked her Daddy for yet another of her good habits: keeping her own unusual supplies hidden away inside her car rather than in a bag or suitcase. "I was around that kind of stuff so much as a kid I never thought much about it."

"Then I wonder if you'd mind if I took a quick look around." Deputy Salyers looked at Cat, but the words were clearly meant to unsettle Tansy. "Just to satisfy my curiosity you might say."

Despite her earlier calm, now Tansy very much wanted to ask a lot more questions. Mainly whether Deputy Salyers had a warrant in hand.

But Cat only smiled and got to her feet.

"I don't mind one bit, Deputy. I don't know much about explosives myself, but I don't think I've got anything like that laying around."

When Deputy Salyers stood and turned toward the kitchen, Cat stared at Tansy, then pointed at the coffee table.

Toward Tansy's cell phone.

Instead of carelessly thrown down with the keys and everything else, now the phone was lined up with the edge of the table. And the barest edge of a white card showed underneath.

Tansy waited long enough for Cat and Deputy Salyers to walk into the kitchen before she grabbed the phone, along with Lori Jane's card underneath.

She didn't have time to call, and she wasn't about to talk about Lee with a cop not far away in a tiny apartment. Instead she pulled up a text message and entered the phone number.

*Lee Couch and box, old Harbury Place. Damn Shrewd One here right now.*

Not the cleverest or most informative message in the world, but all she could come up with on short notice. Before she could worry about Lori Jane not having her phone or being asleep, a reply buzzed in.

*Figures that old asshole would wrangle his way in. Surprised he's still breathing. Under control. Sit tight.*

Tansy bit back a disgusted laugh at Lee's reputation going decades back and way beyond her family, but she wasn't surprised, either. She concentrated on following Cat's low-key chatter through the kitchen, as if she was welcoming a long-lost friend instead of a smart cop getting way too damn close to the truth.

When the voices moved closer, she started to put the phone and card back in her pocket. The memory of Deputy Salyers paying close attention to every small detail in the room stopped her cold. Instead, Tansy arranged them both back on the table, hoping she got it close enough to pass.

The deputy was too tight on Cat's heels for Tansy to give any kind of sign.

"Looks like you've been sleeping out here, Miss Stidham," Deputy Salyers said, glancing at the folded sheets on the back of the couch. "Got any bags or suitcases with you? And would you mind if I took a quick look at them?"

A burst of dialog from the kinds of police and detective shows Cat apparently knew quite well went through Tansy's mind, along with the suggestion that she should demand to have an attorney present. Or at the very least to see a search warrant.

The kinds of things that would look every bit as guilty as showing up for her first interview down at the station with a lawyer by her side.

"Not much, but they're all right there in that closet. Go right on ahead and—"

A weird blip from what looked like a small CB radio mic near Deputy Salyers' shoulder got everyone's attention.

At a muffled voice from the tiny speaker, the deputy turned and strode into the kitchen, leaving Tansy free to flash a quick thumbs-up in Cat's direction. If Lori Jane had enough pull and presence of mind to get the cops into action that fast, they might just manage to catch Lee right where Tansy wanted him.

Deputy Salyers came back out at nearly a run, which was a neat trick in such a small space.

"I'm going to guess neither one of you will mind if I cut this short. Miss Stidham, what was the name of the person you mentioned before? The one your father may have taught."

Tansy made a show of scratching her jaw and staring up at the ceiling.

"I know for sure his first name was Lee..." She let her eyes wander to her brick-hard bed for the last few days. "I think his last name might have been Couch."

Deputy Salyers nodded, already on her way out the door.

"Thank you for your time." Deputy Salyers slammed the door on the way out, and a few seconds later Tansy heard the SUV's big engine fire up.

Cat held still for two painfully long breaths before she darted over to the window and pulled the flimsy curtain back.

"She lit out like she got a wasp's nest snuggled against her backside. Doubt she's the only one headed for the old Harbury place with her ass on fire, either." Cat turned to Tansy, holding her elbows and looking equal parts worried and excited. "Won't Lee just tell them we gave him the stuff and sent him out there?"

Tansy covered her mouth long enough to blow out a breath through her fingers.

"Probably. If he gets the chance. But think about it, Cat. Neither one of us has much of a record to speak of, and Lee's spent his whole miserable life causing trouble for one kind of authority or another. His truck smelled like a rolling distillery, too. Did you touch anything when you put it into that box?"

Cat snorted. "Course I didn't. It's been in that box since you crashed out the other night, soon as we got back here. And I wore gloves the whole time. You're saying his fingerprints are all over that junk, and none of ours are."

"You got it. I honestly hate to say this with all the trouble that's come from our grand scheme so far, but Lee's not the kind to stay calm and reasonable when he sees blue lights in his rear view. He might just do everyone who ever crossed paths with him a favor and get himself into worse trouble than anything we could manage."

"Hell Tansy, I reckon we're due some good luck for a change. Think you ought to call Lori Jane and see how it's going? Or if we need to do anything else?"

"I doubt she'd want to hear from me just yet." Tansy's phone vibrated just as she pulled it out of her pocket. "But I've been wrong plenty of times before, even before I decided it was a good idea to visit my quiet little hometown and get reacquainted with my good buddy Cat Maybell."

Cat flipped the finger in Tansy's direction, but the phone's screen took up a lot more of her attention.

*Cavalry en route to OHP. DSO departed?*

"What's she mean by all that?" Cat peered over Tansy's shoulder.

"I'm gonna guess she got my message, then passed it along to the cops as a hot tip from her imaginary old friend. And that Lee's heading directly into an unfriendly welcome party."

*Departed. Next?*

"So what do we do now, Tansy?"

Despite a surging case of nerves from the number of things that could still go wrong, Tansy smiled.

"I'm hoping Lori Jane has that covered. Cause I got no freaking idea."

Cat gave a strange frown—one that sent uneasy ripples of goosebumps along Tansy's arms—then she walked into the kitchen almost as fast as Deputy Salyers had walked out. She returned with two bright pink shot glasses and an unmarked bottle of something clear, still frosty from the freezer.

"Well, I say we take our chance to relax for a couple minutes before all hell breaks loose again. And I guess now I really ought to tell you what happened with Vickie's knife."

Tansy took one of the shot glasses and stared at it while Cat poured clear, slightly thick liquid into it. A light aroma of maple syrup floated toward her nose.

Instead of asking the question screaming through her mind, she fell back to ones she thought she knew the answer to.

"Moonshine? From Maple Gap?"

Cat grinned and held her little glass up for Tansy to tap with her own.

"You got it. Once I figured out how to get it for myself without having to beg someone else to sell it to me at twice the price, I never go without at least one bottle in my fridge. Worth all the trouble and then some."

Tansy breathed deep, getting a stronger hit of what she'd always loved on her Sunday morning pancakes growing up. And what she remembered tasting on a few special occasions when the adults weren't paying enough attention to notice.

The moonshine went down smooth as silk. Not even a little bit sweet, but still tasting of fine maple syrup all the same.

"Okay. Now tell me."

# CHAPTER 31

CAT TOSSED her own shot of maple moonshine back, then got busy looking everywhere in the tiny living room that wasn't at Tansy.

"Well, I got to thinking about how you said that knife had as much of your blood on it as Vickie's. This was back there at the pot mine when I grabbed it up. So while you were down at the police station talking to Deputy Salyers the first time, I decided to clean it. You know, since that boiler in the basement can't get rid of metal even going full blast in the middle of winter. Scrubbed it real good so it looks like new. I used bleach and an old toothbrush and everything. Helped keep me from staying so nervous, to tell you the truth."

Tansy nodded, no longer sure if the story Cat was working up to telling was going to help or hurt them. Cat poured fragrant new shots for both of them, which didn't clear things up at all.

"Wasn't sure what to do with it then. I figured I would

carry it out to a dump a good ways off from here whenever I got the chance. But you know better than me how fast things got downright crazy. Anyway, just to keep it safe and out of sight, I put it back with the other stuff. Everything we got from the museum."

"Do you mean the stuff from the museum that's still here, Cat? Or the box you handed over to Lee?"

Cat's gaze darted to Tansy's for a hot second before she drained her second teeny glass of moonshine.

"Had it with the gold record, at first. But then when Lee talked to you and me that way, every bit as mean and nasty as you said he'd be, I marched right in here and put it in the bottom of the box. I never did take kindly to an asshole like that trying to threaten me or friends of mine. He's out running the roads with it in his truck right this minute."

Tansy sipped her moonshine a lot more slowly, concentrating on the traces of maple-flavored fire from her lips all the way down to her belly. Giving her thoughts a chance to settle and sort themselves out.

With the way Cat had shifted to staring at her with the wary focus of an actual cat hoping for a smelly treat, but worried about a squirt of cold water, she decided to think out loud instead.

"All right, so he's got the knife. Which should be clear of all the blood and fingerprints. Except maybe for Vickie's since she wasn't wearing gloves that night and we both were. He won't have a chance in hell of knowing what it is. And since Vickie wasn't the one who got cut, the cops won't know what it is, either. Not unless she stole it from someone else like she did the car."

Cat let out her maple-scented breath and closed her eyes for a second.

"Good. I was real worried you'd be mad at me about that part. Too bad he doesn't have the gun, huh? Unless they'd know it was yours."

Tansy shook her head.

"They might, but it would be pretty damn tough to track down. My Daddy told me plenty of times after he gave it to me that he never did inform our fine Commonwealth of Virginia about buying that one, or giving it to me. I've spent the most time in Georgia, and they don't have any kind of firearm registration. Is the gun still here?"

"Sure is. Safe and sound with the rest."

Tansy sat forward, resting her elbows on her knees. She wasn't sure whether the movement or talking about the knife caused it, but the slice on her side flexed and pulled like pure fire.

"Might be a good idea to show me that hiding place of yours. In case I get that call from Lori Jane and need to get to it—"

Both of them half jumped out of their skins when an ear-splitting siren wail started low and rose up banshee-high, partly because it sounded like it was about twenty feet away.

"What the *hell* is that?" Tansy shouted, clapping her hands to her ears.

Cat jumped up and yanked the curtain to the side.

"Fire siren! Hardly ever goes off anymore since most of the volunteers got cell phones and such now! Got to be an emergency, or..."

She dropped the curtain and turned toward Tansy, hand on her chest.

The siren slowly wound down, leaving Tansy's ears ringing and her heart pounding.

"Could they be doing that because of something like a car crash?" she whispered. She felt a faint twinge of guilt for what she was thinking, but nowhere near as deep as she had about Vickie. "You know, like a police chase that went real wrong?"

Cat nodded. "It's happened before. I don't know if your folks ever had those old police-band scanners sitting around in the kitchen, but I sure do wish we had one right now." She scurried to the coffee table and grabbed her huge cell phone. "Might find something online though. Not as fast, mind you, but this here's the next best thing."

Tansy tried not to stare at her own phone's black screen, since trying to will Lori Jane to reply to her text was more likely to drive Tansy crazy than make a little blue speech bubble magically appear.

But the surface lit up at the same time Cat gasped.

"Single vehicle crash, out toward the old Harbury place..."

*Stay put. Things happening fast.*

Tansy squeezed her eyes closed, torn between hoping for the best outcome for her and Cat, and the fierce internal scolding from every preacher, pastor, and Sunday School teacher her grandparents had forced her to listen to as a little girl.

Cat leaned over and grabbed Tansy's arm. Her voice came out whispery and thin.

"It says rescue squad on the way, but police already there. You don't think it could be him, do you?"

Forcing herself to look at Cat, Tansy shrugged and shivered at the same time.

"I never did go in for all the superstitions I heard growing up, like throwing salt over your shoulder or not ever saying your wishes out loud. But in this case, I'm not saying one *word* until I know what's going on."

Cat stared at Tansy, eyes wide and face getting paler.

"My Mamaw always said anything I wished bad on another person would come back on me a whole lot worse. I thought it was funny back then, like she was too backwards to know how much she sounded like a witch. Her friends down at the Baptist church never would have got over that kind of talk. I'm with you right now, though. I don't like it, but I'm gonna wait and see."

Tansy held up her phone, and while Cat read it buzzed in her hand.

"Better take a look, Tansy."

*Box important? May not be recoverable.*

Tansy's fingers shook enough when she tried to tap out a reply that she kept having to back up and start over.

*Important stuff safe. You okay?*

"She must know one of the cops or the rescue squad a lot better than she let on," Cat said. "To find out so fast. She's running ahead of the website for sure."

"She might *be* there for all we know." Tansy didn't say it out loud, but she couldn't stop wondering just how involved Lori Jane truly was.

*Okay. Couch trouble may be over. Bad idea to run.*

"Does she mean bad for Lee to run, or for us to?" Cat said in a shaky voice. "I don't know about you, but I'm gonna need another hit of this moonshine before I get more tore up than your Auntie Louise over all this waiting."

Tansy nodded, wishing herself that she could speed up time, or maybe fall asleep and wake up to find the whole thing over with.

Her nerves were generally steady—they had to be, with all the things her Daddy taught her that she still got up to from time to time.

But waiting for so many things entirely outside of her control to find their conclusions didn't suit her even a little bit.

She managed to tap out a message without so much shaking this time.

*Sitting tight. Here when needed.*

"I imagine we're in for a while at this point." She put her phone down face-side up and shook out her hands and fingers. "Sounds to me like anyone who might have been looking at us has their hands full right now. I say we settle in and get ready to lay low for a while."

Cat handed Tansy's pink shot glass back, so full this time the liquid was level with the edge.

She didn't spill a drop when she swallowed it down.

The two of them sat cross-legged on the scratchy brick sofa, staring at the blank television.

Waiting.

# CHAPTER 32

THEY'D GONE through another shot—followed by Cat wandering into the kitchen for big glasses of milk and peanut butter and jelly sandwiches to soak up some of the booze, another of their long-ago munchie traditions—before Tansy finally decided to turn the TV on.

The gathering out-of-town news folks must have been disappointed when drama they were counting on from Captain O'Quinn's widow never materialized.

Or bored. Or ordered to get some kind of story to make up for the cost of hauling themselves way out to the ass-end of Vail County.

Because three different regional networks were showing their own aerial footage of a floodlight- and headlight-brightened mountain road, which the glaring headline at the bottom of the screen declared was Route 37 not far outside of Craigen. A sure sign of at least those news crews coming equipped with drones they were bound and damned determined to use.

Tansy didn't have to look at any kind of map to know Route 37 was the road to the old Harbury place.

The normally quiet, pale-gray asphalt road twisting through a bunch of big trees with their bright spring leaves barely visible with all the light on the ground was packed full of police cars from more than one little town, and white news vans each painted with vivid logos from their home stations.

While the two of them watched with their mouths dropped open, the current channel's drone floated down from the night sky to follow the lumbering progress of an ambulance arriving on the scene. Not in any kind of hurry, either.

The lights were spinning on top, but Tansy knew before Cat turned up the volume that the siren wouldn't be making a sound.

Because none of the cops standing around the smoking mess of a pickup truck that had launched itself off the side of one of the curves were close enough to be trying to get the driver out. All they did was hold high-beam flashlights.

From the looks of the long, swerving black marks on the pale asphalt, the truck's impact with a stand of three huge trees had been fast enough to stop anyone from worrying overly much about survivors.

A red-cheeked kid reporting for a station about an hour-and-a-half away chattered on about the driver running from a simple traffic stop. From the way he told it, a patrol car stopped to investigate a vehicle parked by the side of the road. Taillights out, dome light on.

The driver took off before the cop got out of the car.

And didn't stop until the trees stopped him.

Cat pulled her feet up onto the couch, arms wrapped around her knees.

"Does that sound real to you?"

Tansy didn't look away from the screen. Her own arms crawled with almost painful gooseflesh.

"I wouldn't put it past Lee to run like that, no. Sounds like him to pull over, get a fresh drink or two, and see what kind of goodies he threatened us out of. But it doesn't exactly *feel* real. Know what I mean?"

"Yeah," Cat whispered. "I know. Can't quite say how I feel myself."

Tansy knew her phone buzzed in her pocket, but she would have sworn her leg was attached to someone else. She fumbled with that other person's fingers trying to get ahold of it, and finally unlocked the screen.

*Got a place where I can hide for a bit? Need a break. And to talk.*

She held the phone out toward Cat.

Both of them burst into nervous laughter.

At least in Tansy's case, relief twisted up with booze and a dose of sick guilt to leave her more woozy than a few shots of moonshine could account for.

"Have her come on by," Cat said, wiping her eyes. "Might want to park somewhere else just to be safe, but she might as well join the party."

Lori Jane showed up quick enough that Tansy wondered all over again whether she'd been out there when the wreck happened, or if she just had a very close and very chatty contact with the police.

The sight of her in Cat's tiny, shabby living room only turned up the sense of unreality.

Surely no one with such smooth, gleaming blonde-streaked-with-silver hair pulled back into a loose ponytail that showed off those sparkling diamond earrings should ever set foot in such humble surroundings. Especially not when those feet wore low boots of a soft burgundy leather that matched her short leather jacket over the same shimmering black outfit she'd worn before.

But Lori Jane showed her local roots when she zeroed in on the shot glasses still sitting on the coffee table. And her voice and accent slipped right back into pure Vail County.

"Got any more of whatever you been drinking? Smells like local high-test to me. I sure could use something to take the edge off."

She sat in one of Cat's chairs with a heavy sigh, then leaned forward and plopped a hand-sized black leather case with gold accents on the coffee table. Her voice went back to big-city normal.

"I brought plenty of my own to share, of course. But I'd welcome a little taste of home on a night like this."

Cat stared for a second, still standing by the closed front door. She shook herself and fluffed her perm-curls a little higher.

"Why sure, I've got plenty set back. Enough that me and Tansy couldn't put it all away without laying ourselves passed out on the floor."

Tansy smiled and waved one hand toward Lori Jane.

"Lori Jane Holbrook, also known as Mrs. O'Quinn, meet my old friend Cat Maybell. Cat, this here's Lori Jane."

Lori Jane leaned forward with her hand out, gleaming manicured pink nails shining in the television's shifting light.

Cat stared again as if a big copperhead snake had appeared in her very own living room.

"Nice to meet you, Cat."

"Oh, nice to meet you too, Missus O'Quinn, ma'am." Cat darted forward and grabbed Lori Jane's hand, shaking it with a little too much energy. "I'll be right back with a glass for you."

Lori Jane's laugh was low and smooth as the moonshine.

"If we're sharing your best 'shine and my best weed, I'll insist you call me Lori Jane. And I wouldn't mind a little bit bigger glass if you've got one."

Cat nodded and bobbed down into a passing imitation of an honest-to-goodness curtsey, leaving Tansy biting her cheeks to stop from laughing.

"Sure thing, Lori Jane," Cat called over her shoulder on the way to the kitchen.

Tansy and Lori Jane took their turns staring at each other, with only the low mutter from the TV to break the silence.

"Want me to turn that thing off?" Tansy said.

Lori Jane nodded with a tired smile.

"I wouldn't argue if you did. We're not going to learn anything new from the local news, no matter how many vans show up. Or how many of those goddamned drones they send buzzing overhead."

The low electronic click of the TV going dead seemed to echo even in the small room.

Tansy finally took a deep breath and grabbed onto her courage.

"Am I going to learn anything new from you?"

Lori Jane glanced toward the kitchen.

"You both will. I might have just met Cat, but I have no doubt she hears most anything you do. Probably for good reason."

Tansy shook her head. "I'm not going to say—"

Lori Jane held up one hand.

"I'm not criticizing or complaining, Tansy. There are plenty of times I miss having a good friend I've known since I was a kid. Someone who knows me inside and out. The kind you don't bother hiding anything from. Those have been awfully hard to come by for a long time for me, at least anyone from my time living here. Jimmy was the only one left, really."

Going by her own experience of relationships that rarely lasted more than a few months, Tansy had no idea what to say to that.

Thank all the moonshine that flowed through the mountains, Cat hurried back into the living room.

She handed Lori Jane a white coffee cup printed all over with multicolored line drawings of cats.

"From my big brother Ricky." Cat shrugged, cheeks turning bright red. "I hardly ever use it. I think he meant it as a joke gift, but I... Anyway, fill it up however much you want."

She set a full jar of moonshine on the table, still frosty except where the outline of her fingers had melted it.

With the biggest smile Tansy had seen from her, Lori Jane held the mug up and turned it from side to side.

"I'd say your brother has great taste, Cat. I appreciate you letting me use it."

She poured herself a solid double-shot, then filled Tansy and Cat's little pink glasses. All three of them held theirs up.

"To bad situations that turn out the best way they can," Lori Jane said.

Tansy was too confused—and curious—to do anything except toss her shot back. Cat did the same, and Lori Jane swallowed half of hers before closing her eyes and letting out a sigh that smelled like pancakes on a lazy Sunday morning.

"That's a mighty fine batch you've got there, Cat. The kind you can't get outside these mountains. I see why you keep it stocked up." She opened her eyes and carefully put the cup on the coffee table.

"Okay. Not everything made it onto the local news, despite their best efforts. That *was* Lee Couch in the crash, and I'm not too broken up about him no longer stalking the earth. He was right there egging my asshole family and their friends on to treat me like shit back when the museum opened."

The cursing sounded strange in that level, rich-city-dweller accent, but the venom behind it made perfect sense.

"That's exactly the kind of thing he loves most." Tansy shook her head. She wasn't anywhere near ready to think about playing a big part in two people ending up dead in just a couple days' time. "*Loved* most, I guess I should say. I'm not sure how I feel about that yet."

Lori Jane picked up her little black case from the coffee table and unzipped it. Inside was the dainty water pipe she'd shared with Tansy the night they met. It was miles away from the cheap things Tansy, Cat, and their disreputable friends had passed around back in school.

This was finely made, with silvery metal fittings covered in delicate scrollwork. A rounded metal case tucked into the red velvet lining beside the pipe was just as elaborately decorated with similar designs.

"Anyone interested?" Lori Jane said. "I've got more to tell."

"I'd take a hit or two," Tansy said. "It's real good weed, Cat."

Cat nodded and got to her feet.

"Count me in. I'll fetch you some water."

# CHAPTER 33

TANSY WATCHED Lori Jane pop the tiny case open and pinch out enough sticky, glistening green buds to fill the pipe's bowl. She took the bottle of water Cat brought out and filled the glass bulb.

"From what I heard," Lori Jane said, "none of the fine officers were surprised when Lee's license plate was called in. What little judgement he ever had apparently deserted him over the last few years. Word was it was only a matter of time before he ended up the way he did tonight. A lot of people in Craigen and all over the county could only hope he didn't take someone out with him."

"The news said he was parked by the side of the road," Cat said. "Then he ran from the cops."

Lori Jane nodded as she spun the wheel on a very old-fashioned metal lighter. The refillable kind Tansy had last seen her grandfather use. The yellow flame flashed the marijuana into glowing orange embers.

After a slow inhale that bubbled hot smoke through cooling water, Lori Jane held her breath and passed the pipe to Cat.

"Run he did," Lori Jane said on her cloudy exhale. "Before the officer could even put the cruiser in park, Lee took off. Nothing is official yet, but sounds like the interior of his truck reeked of whiskey. And nothing as good as what you so generously shared with me. He fired up the engine and stomped the gas but never got control before he got acquainted with those trees. Even then, he might have been banged up but alive if he'd bothered with his seatbelt. They were able to rescue the box, by the way. Got word right before I knocked on your door."

Cat exhaled and passed the pipe to Tansy.

"Good," Tansy said. "I'm glad the museum will get that stuff back. And the rest of it, of course."

She took a hit off the still-glowing embers.

Lori Jane raised one finely shaped eyebrow.

"This isn't likely to make it into the media for a while, if ever. But everyone sure is wondering where the knife came from."

Tansy coughed and swore at the same time.

"Look at me choking like a damn kid." She took a few swallows from the water bottle to try and get the burning tickle in her throat under control. "I'd guess that knife belonged to my cousin Vickie, but I can't say for sure."

Lori Jane nodded with a half-smile.

"It's often hard to say in situations like this, isn't it? Anyway, thankfully the officer who spotted Lee's truck was from Craigen. That way they get to claim solving the case, even if all they did was pull over to investigate why someone was sitting in a pickup truck not quite all the way off a narrow road. Saying they caught him matters. Even if he did catch himself in the end."

Tansy was still too busy clearing her throat to say anything, so she was relieved when Cat jumped in. The way Lori Jane kept watching was unnerving.

"The cops got a good tip on where the possible thief was heading, huh?"

Tansy finally relaxed her shoulders and caught a good deep breath when Lori Jane turned her green eyes toward Cat.

"Yeah, turns out a high school friend of mine from way back heard the gossip they needed, and was a good enough citizen to pass the word along. My insurance company will be quite pleased tomorrow when I let them know. Just like Deputy Salyers was when *she* heard Lee knew his way around explosives. That was the main thing that had them chasing their tails about what happened. It sure is funny how everything worked out for the best."

This time when Lori Jane gazed at her, Tansy decided she had to speak up. Nothing like a full confession, mind you, or enough honesty to get herself or Cat into any more trouble than they already had.

But she was afraid keeping quiet about two people who would soon be under the ground—no matter how she truly felt about those people—would end up haunting her in the middle of the night.

She already had enough sleepless nights in store to take a chance on sending more her way. Even if saying her piece led straight to more questions she didn't want to answer.

"It's good you're getting the stuff back for the museum, Lori Jane, it really is. But I don't know if everyone would call two people over at the funeral home 'things working out for the best.' Not too many folks will shed a tear over Lee or Vickie, I guess, even though my aunt is pretty upset. Still kinda feels strange to call it good."

Lori Jane nodded, again with that odd half-smile, as she picked up her coffee mug.

"You make an excellent point, Tansy. One I can't argue with. So how about we call it working out for the *better* instead? After all, the three of us probably never would have met if no one ever had the original idea to break into the museum."

Tansy heard Cat's quick breath beside her. But she'd learned more than explosives from her Daddy all those years ago, especially when it came to situations that could get real bad, real quick.

She started right back into Lori Jane's eyes.

"You're right," Tansy said. "And that would have been a damn shame. Despite all your years in Nashville with the country music crowd, I think we got sort of a common way of looking at the world."

"I do believe you're right about that." Lori Jane swallowed the rest of her moonshine and sighed. "Maybe it's a bit like this fine beverage. The kind of thing you never really find outside these mountains."

Tansy picked up the water pipe, waiting for Lori Jane to pass her the lighter. After taking a long hit and holding her breath for a less-embarrassing amount of time, she breathed out cool, sweetish smoke.

"The kind of thing that might make you want to look out for each other is what I say. Even when mistakes get made, 'cause they're always going to."

She gave the pipe and lighter to Lori Jane, getting a full smile in return.

"*Especially* when mistakes get made. I've made plenty in my time. And the people I'm most grateful to are the ones who gave me a chance to learn. You know, kept me from getting myself into serious trouble until I managed to get my thick, empty head out of my own dumb ass."

A laugh snorted its way out of Cat, and Tansy couldn't keep herself from smiling.

"I've got more than my fair share of trouble keeping my head out of my ass," Cat said. "Not sure I learn from every one, but I keep trying."

Lori Jane kept watching Tansy, but she still looked more curious and amused than angry.

Time to take a chance.

"Now that we've shared our dope and moonshine, why don't you go ahead and say what you want to, Lori Jane. I can see something simmering away in your eyes brighter than that lighter of yours."

Lori Jane flicked the lighter on again, then adjusted the flame high enough that it sputtered, then back down to a reasonable level.

"That's one thing I've liked about you since we first met, Tansy. You're willing to get right down to business and do what it takes to get the job done." She flipped the lighter closed. "Now that we're all here and talking, do we need to keep up the game? As in driving all the way out to the old Harbury place? Assuming we could even get out there tonight, since the road is blocked by the solution to one of our shared problems and all."

For a quick second, Tansy thought about trying to talk to Cat alone, like they had with Lee. The hiding place was Cat's secret, after all, and hers to share or not.

But with Lee it *had* been a game. One that turned out to have much more serious consequences than Tansy expected.

Maybe she'd played enough games in her life. More than enough for one visit home.

"We don't have to drive all the way out there," she said. "I'd say it's up to Cat whether she wants to let us see where the stuff is. But I figure we should send it back where it belongs no matter what."

Cat stared at Tansy for a few seconds, eyebrows drawn down into a scowl.

"This part is up to you, Cat, it really is," Tansy said. "All I know is we've had way more luck—good and bad—than we deserve. I'm afraid the balance is sure to tip the wrong way on us right quick if we don't stop."

Now Cat's raised eyebrows revealed a collection of fine lines on her forehead, a whole lot like the ones Tansy had seen in the mirror that morning.

Could be they were both getting too old for this kind of nonsense.

Just look where it got Vickie. And Lee.

Cat held up both hands.

"I'm not about to argue with you. I reckon my next move is to get the hell out of town one way or the other, so no need to keep this dump's secrets. Time to grow up, move out, and move on."

She lowered her hands and smacked her own thighs before she stood and headed into the kitchen. Lori Jane looked at Tansy with both eyebrows raised.

"I have no earthly idea what she's got back there," Tansy said. "We'll both be learning something new. But I do know you can trust her."

Lori Jane stood and held out one hand toward the door Cat had just walked through.

"After you, then. I wouldn't be here if I didn't trust both of you. And I do love to get in on a juicy secret."

# CHAPTER 34

CAT WASN'T in the main part of the kitchen, near the cheap but gleaming clean countertop or appliances. She'd crossed the short stretch of faded yellow linoleum all the way to the little pantry closet—a dark brown door set into the white wall.

When Tansy and Lori Jane crowded in behind her, Cat grinned and opened the door on a green metal box the height of her shoulder and about three feet wide. About all Tansy could tell was the furnace looked brand-new without a trace of the dust or grime or dents she'd always seen on HVAC equipment wherever she'd lived.

No scent of gas or oil or anything else ever burning in there, either.

Every square inch around and above the furnace was lined with bare-wood shelves, holding an impressive array of the kind of quick and cheap food Tansy and everyone else she knew grew up with. Boxes of macaroni and cheese, tins of sardines and tuna, and cans of soup sharing space with chips, boxes of cookies, and jars of all kinds of preserved food from pickles to beets to peaches.

And of course, a row of what looked like the same moonshine they'd been sharing.

"Used to be a lot more room in here before my genius landlord decided to shove a furnace in there," Cat said. "Once we all figured out she wasn't gonna come get the damn things, most everyone else sold them. Didn't get much, because they weren't much to start with. Would have frozen our asses off if we'd let her get away with it. I had a different idea for mine."

She opened the front of the furnace like a door, revealing a pristine white waffly filter at the bottom and a mess of wires on a panel at the top.

Cat pointed at what Tansy thought was a row of yellow circuit breakers on the right.

But when she flipped them all up, the filter, panel and all popped out on that side.

Inside was nothing at all, at least not what any kind of furnace should look like.

Lori Jane let out a low, breathy laugh at the sight of Captain O'Quinn and the Confederates' one and only gold record, safe and sound against the empty metal box of the furnace. The mandolin was in there too, along with the rest of their haul from the museum.

Two shelves along the bottom held Tansy's gun and the rest of their thieving supplies, all as clean and neatly stacked as if they were on display in a fancy department store.

"Not a scratch on it," Lori Jane said as Cat handed the framed gold record to her. "Quite a hiding place you've got there."

"Told you no one would find it, Tansy," Cat said. "I cut the power first, then took my time getting rid of all the stuff inside so no one would catch on. Sold a bunch of it for scrap, the rest for spare parts. Hate to leave it behind, but I figure if I can do this, I can work something out no matter where I land next."

Lori Jane glanced up with a fleeting smile, but her attention was captured by the wooden frame in her hands. She stepped back enough to brace it against the countertop.

"I haven't seen this since the museum opened." Her fingertips traced the outline of the gold disc, then lingered on the little plaque proclaiming "Mountain Deep Heartache" had sold half a million copies. "I've seen a bunch more over the years, including from other people singing Jimmy's songs. Platinum and multi-platinum, too, hanging on the wall in my house in Nashville. But none of them would have meant as much to him as this one. Doesn't mean as much to me, either."

A tear landed on the plaque, and Lori Jane laughed softly. She wiped it away with her sleeve.

Tansy's own eyes burned, and she heard Cat sniff.

"You should have seen him, sitting at the rickety table in our grubby old tour bus, staring at this thing. It was like he couldn't look away for days on end. Everyone in the band took to teasing him—and me—about it, saying he'd found a brand-new girlfriend who would shove all of us to the side and run off with him for good. I was the only one who knew how much it meant to Jimmy. The thing none of us knew was how the weak blood vessel that had been lurking in his brain since he was born would steal him away from all of us years too soon."

Instead of feeling sad, or even sympathetic, Tansy felt more than a little sick to her stomach.

This whole crazy scheme to get a little quick cash had turned out not too terrible in the end, or it seemed like it would so far. Didn't seem like she or Cat would go to jail, or even have to scrounge up buyers. The museum and Lori Jane would get their treasures back, and if Lori Jane kept her word, Tansy and Cat would end up with at least some kind of reward.

But as awful as Vickie and Lee ending up dead was, right now Tansy was flat-out disgusted with herself for deciding no one would care about what got stolen.

Watching Lori Jane caress a fake-gold record inside a wooden frame—the tougher-than-steel music-multi-million-aire now with a freshly re-broken heart—put all the notions of this being a victimless crime to deep shame.

"I'm real sorry about all of this, Lori Jane," Tansy said. "I never should have set foot inside that museum thinking the way I was. Almost everything around me has gone bad since that day."

Cat walked over to the sink and grabbed a flowery paper towel and blew her nose.

"Didn't start that day, Tansy, and you know it. This mess really started the day I snuck up on you down at the river. It was all my rotten idea, remember?"

Lori Jane scooted the frame all the way onto the counter, then retrieved the mandolin. The kitchen's light flashed off the shiny brown surface, with a lighter brown area under eight strings that made it clear this was more than just a miniature guitar.

"Did you read any of the tags at the museum?" She brushed the strings lightly, and the tone rang high and sweet.

Tansy and Cat both shook their heads. Tansy's throat was too tight to say a word. From the way Cat kept swallowing, she wasn't her normal smartass self either.

"This isn't the one Jimmy played on 'Mountain Deep Heartache' or any other recording. That one's at my house and will stay with me until I'm under the ground beside him. I got him this one with the first big royalty check from that song. He played it on tour and showed off to everyone who would listen what a fine instrument his sweetheart gave him. But he never used it to write songs. Said it didn't have the same magic from our barely-getting-by days when we fell in love."

She carefully set the mandolin on top of the gold record before moving to the side enough to lean back against the counter with her arms crossed.

Enough time passed in silence that Tansy moved over to lean against the stove before Cat finally spoke.

"I'm real sorry about everything too, Lori Jane. We busted in all full of wrong ideas and big plans, and it all went wrong pretty much from the start. Sounds kinda dumb right now, but I didn't understand how much other people would get hurt."

Lori Jane nodded with a tight smile.

"Apologies accepted, from both of you. I've made more than enough mistakes in my life to understand how it happens. Me and Jimmy were plenty desperate enough in the early days for me to pretend I don't understand that part too. We got away with more than we deserved to. More than I'm willing to admit to at this point in my life."

Tansy managed to stop herself from chewing on her own lips again.

"Thank you, Lori Jane. I guess it's way past time for me to get my ass out of town before I break anything else. I still think you ought to head out with me, Cat. See what we can't get into with a change of scenery."

Cat wiped at her eyes and smiled.

"Been feeling like I'm way overdue for some kind of reset myself. I might just take you up on that." She squinted at Lori Jane. "You ain't gonna turn us in for what we did? Couldn't argue with you if you did."

"I'm not going to turn you in. And I plan to keep my word to Tansy about sending you on your way with a good-sized nest egg. I owe you that much for helping me keep this out of the music-media cesspool. Like I said, I haven't told you or anyone else some of the crazy things me and Jimmy had to do back when we were starting out. I know exactly how tough it is to break loose from hard times, especially when you start out about half underwater. Having some rag's ambitious gossip reporter of the week dig a bunch of that up would redefine nightmare for me."

Lori Jane gave that odd half-smile again and shook her head.

"Anyway, I had the unbelievable good luck of hooking up with one of the best songwriters these mountains ever produced, and that's a tough contest. I'm not lying when I say I hope you two can make different choices from here on out."

Tansy wasn't sure whether her warm lightheadedness was because of Lori Jane's words or her weed, but she didn't much care.

For once in her life, getting a second chance she didn't deserve meant more to her than one she'd earned.

"Well, can I offer you a jar of 'shine to take back to Nashville with you?" Cat grabbed a fresh one from her furnace-pantry and held it out. "It ain't much I know, but I feel like I got to do something for you."

Lori Jane nodded once and took the jar.

"It's a lot more than you know, Cat. And no matter what you started out meaning to get for yourselves—or who ended up on the wrong side of events for their trouble—you two ended up doing me a favor. I doubt I'll ever feel at home here again for more reasons than I care to think about. But it's done me a world of good to see how many folks really do care about Captain O'Quinn and the Confederates. I won't forget that again."

"Do you need anything else that we can do?" Tansy said. "Maybe something that *doesn't* involve you having to rush back here and help a couple of bargain basement crooks clean up their damn mess?"

"Grab that mandolin for me?" Lori Jane picked up the gold record herself. "And anything else that needs to go back to the museum? Just help me get it loaded in my car and I'll take it from there." She started toward the living room, then stopped and turned around.

"And maybe drop me a text sometime. Let me know where you fetch up. You probably heard a big part of what I do now is help folks in Nashville get a leg up before the studio system chews them up and spits them out. I guess I like knowing how my special projects turn out in the end."

"You got it," Tansy said. "We'll do our best to send you some good news."

# CHAPTER 35

TANSY TUCKED the last thing from Cat's apartment—a huge Tupperware container full of her Auntie Louise's incredible maple fudge—into the only empty space left in her car.

Cat's car was every bit as full, but they'd managed to pack everything worth taking in only a couple of days.

After almost a week of waiting around for Vickie's funeral, getting back on the road was the only thing Tansy could imagine doing next.

Neither her aunt nor anyone else walking around in the world could convince her to go to Lee's planting in a couple of days.

The morning was bright and sunny, with more than a little heat to make it clear June was closer than anyone was ready for. More people than usual were out strolling the streets of Craigen, and all of them seemed to be in a mood as cheery and pleasant as the day.

One of the restaurants not too far away was baking the

proper Appalachian cornbread Tansy and Cat were both going to miss.

They'd be on the way to Atlanta before a scrap of it came out of the oven.

Cat's bruises had healed, most of the soreness was finally gone from Tansy's shoulder, and all her cuts and scrapes seemed to be taking care of themselves just fine. Even the slice across her ribs had knitted well enough that it only hurt if she moved just right.

A fine, clear day for driving had them almost as cheerful as everyone else in town. Cat didn't even fuss all that much at having to keep it relatively close to the speed limit on the way down south.

She locked the apartment's door and dropped the key into the rectangular black mailbox beside it, then grinned at Tansy.

"Doubt they'll find anyone as interesting as me to rent this dump to. Not that I plan to give much of a shit once we put this town in our rearview."

"The last place I had in Atlanta wasn't exactly a palace," Tansy said. "But I reckon we can do a little bit better for ourselves if we stick together."

Cat stared at her for a second, obviously trying to decide whether Tansy was joking or serious. Tansy had the feeling some part of Cat kept waiting to hear the whole move was off, and she'd have to fend for herself and try to start all over again in their little hometown. Including worrying about the police eventually figuring their whole misadventure out.

"I guess I'm set up a good bit better than most folks leaving home for the first time," Cat finally said. "Between having you to show me the ropes and Mrs. O'Quinn's contribution. Might even give me time to figure out what kind of work I might be suited for down in that big city instead of taking the first crappy job I can find."

Even though Lori Jane had indeed left town the morning after retrieving the gold record and everything else from Cat's furnace-safe, two envelopes had shown up later that same afternoon. Hand-delivered by a woman in comfortably worn jeans and a blue Tennessee Titans shirt who still managed to put Tansy one-hundred percent on edge.

Something about the calm, quiet woman somehow screamed what a huge mistake it would be to give her any trouble, or even think about it.

Someone would *have* to be that way to carry around enough cash to buy a good-sized house in Vail County and not break a sweat. The money wouldn't get them nearly as far in Atlanta, but it would certainly take the edge off in about a hundred different ways.

"You won't be alone in trying to figure out what to do next," Tansy said. "I don't exactly have any of my big set of plans worked out for myself just yet. I just hope it makes a hell of a lot more sense than my last set did."

Cat snorted, then took a sharp look at something behind Tansy.

"Your favorite local cop just showed up to give you a big goodbye hug. Want me to hang around?"

Tansy didn't have to turn to know Cat meant Deputy Salyers. The last few days had kept all the town and county cops too busy to care much about following up leads that seemed to go nowhere.

But Tansy knew this was one officer who was too damn good to forget her entirely accurate suspicions.

"I guess you'll have to," she said, "now that you technically don't live here anymore. Unless you want to fish that key back out and stand around in an empty apartment."

Deputy Salyers was on foot this time, still in uniform, crossing the parking lot without a trace of the urgency she'd shown heading out when she got the call about Lee. Her skin was too dark to show it, but Tansy would have bet the puffiness under her eyes was the result of nowhere near enough sleep for a few days.

"Morning, Deputy," Tansy said, aware lack of sleep wouldn't likely dull the risk here. "Surprised to see you out so early."

Standing with her hands on her hips, Deputy Salyers nodded.

"Getting back to my normal schedule isn't my favorite thing to do after several days of working overnights. Looks like you two are heading somewhere."

"Figured I might want to see a little bit more than Vail County for a change," Cat said. "Got all my rent and utilities taken care of if that's why you're here."

"I guess you both know that's not why I'm here. Just as much as you believe I can't do much of anything about it. And maybe I can't. We'll see, won't we?"

Tansy smiled, doing her best to keep it from twisting into a nervous grin. She wouldn't have minded putting Craigen firmly in her rearview without crossing paths with Deputy Salyers again.

"I'm not about to guess what brought you this way," Tansy

said. "I get the feeling you're the kind to let me know right quick, whether I guess or not."

"I suppose I wanted to let you know you've made an impression, Ms. Stidham. Same as you did, Ms. Maybell. One I won't soon forget. No matter how happy some of my co-workers might be to call this a closed case and move on to things with a lot less potential negative publicity."

She watched Tansy and Cat, almost like she was waiting for one of them to twitch the wrong way or let out an incriminating giggle.

Tansy wished she wasn't quite so worried about that happening herself.

"I trust you'll drive carefully on your way down to Georgia," Deputy Salyers said once the silence played out long enough to suit her. "Probably best for everyone involved if you settle down there or somewhere else far away from this corner of Virginia and stay put."

She touched the brim of her hat with two fingers and walked away.

Once she was far enough away to be out of hearing range, Cat bumped Tansy's shoulder with her own.

"Lord, Tansy, she wanted to haul our asses in so bad *I* could taste it. Think she's gonna keep checking on us until we do something dumb enough to set the cops in Atlanta on us?"

"All I'm gonna say is we better keep our damn noses clean so she can't find anything to dig into. That and hope she gets promoted out of here so quick she won't have a chance to worry about us. She's good enough that I doubt it will take long."

Cat shivered all over and fluffed her permed curls into a fluffier arrangement.

"Ready to head out?"

Tansy grinned and shook her head.

"Not just yet. Got one more stop in mind that will give us all the information we need to know exactly what we're leaving behind. Meet me at the Drop In and Shop and we'll get road-trip junk food for our cars and ourselves while we're at it."

# CHAPTER 36

THE CROWD at the convenience store was a lot bigger than the day Tansy had run into Lee and helped set his eventual end in motion. But none of the Grouchy Old Men's Hot Dog Committee was in attendance, thank goodness. Mostly the last straggling groups of distracted people rushing to get kids to school and themselves to work on time. The ones running late enough that they had no chance of making it.

That suited Tansy just fine. Hardly anyone would have time to pay attention to her.

The ones who mattered were there, though, and not pulling frantic-caffeine-and-snack-seeker duty for the line at the front counter. A couple of surly kids who had to be fresh out of school years themselves were holding that part of the operation down.

Her gossip buddies Mark and Tim were busy stocking a surprisingly empty beer cooler for a Wednesday morning. Tim stepped out from the little door leading inside the cooler, pulling a blue toboggan off his head that looked a hell of a lot less scratchy and smelly than the masks Cat had provided for the museum robbery.

He waved toward Tansy, his curly mostly-gray hair just about as fluffy as Cat's from the static.

"Tansy! Heard you were headed out of town. I knew you wouldn't hit the road without stopping in to say goodbye."

Mark waved through the empty space for the basically no-name beer that always sold best. He stepped out rubbing his now-red bald spot.

"How on earth can you stand to be in there without a hat or something?" Tansy said. "I'm getting the chills just looking at you."

"I think I might have babied my hair too much when I was a kid," Mark said. "Maybe if I try to toughen it up, the rest won't run off on me. Speaking of run off, where you headed? Back down south?"

"Yeah, gonna give Atlanta another try with a better attitude. At least that's my plan. Cat's out there gassing up her rolling metal death trap."

Tim peered out the window, trying to smooth his hair but only giving it more of a staticky crackle.

"I sure hope it's a good change of pace for both of you. Not that you'll get near as much excitement as you do right here at home. Been keeping up with all the latest?"

Tansy laughed and turned to grab a couple of bags of potato chips to hide her face for a second.

"Not near as well as I should, I'm sure. What's the good word?"

Mark picked up a clipboard off a stack of cases of beer, peered at it for a second, then let out a much put-upon sigh.

"I don't know if you'd call much of it *good*, not unless you're trying to stop everyone from yanking their stuff out of that museum once it got busted into. About as far as I'd go is calling it better than it was."

Tansy frowned. "I thought that all got settled down once they figured out who was involved. Or was that just people wishing it so at my cousin's funeral the other day?"

Tim leaned over and smacked Mark on the shoulder.

"Real nice bringing that up in front of Tansy, Mark."

Mark's face turned as red as his bald spot, and he tossed the clipboard down with a clatter.

"Oh shit, I'm sorry. Sometimes I get to running my mouth and forget who I'm talking to. Looks like the museum is going to be okay, though, so that's good, right?"

Tim jumped in with a glare at his longtime gossip buddy.

"Well yeah, I'd call that part good. All that missing stuff turned back up, not a scratch on any of it. Wait, you *did* hear about Lee Couch, didn't you? I don't want to go springing something else on you on top of the rest."

Tansy let out a sigh, staring down at the faded but spotlessly clean red and yellow tiles.

"All I heard is he might have been the one thieving with Vickie that night. After the way that asshole treated my Daddy and the rest of us, that wouldn't surprise me one tiny bit."

Mark glanced around at the mostly empty store, apparently recovered from his embarrassment at Tim's swat. No one else was inside except Cat, up front chatting with the kids behind the counter. Giving Tansy time to get the real news.

Exactly as she and Tansy had worked out before they got there.

"Word is they're not a *hundred* percent sure if he was thieving with her or figured it out later, but it's looking more and more like he's the one who... You know. Anyway, some folks think someone *else* might have been involved too. Because an anonymous call tipped the cops off on where Lee was that night he crashed his truck."

Tim smirked in a not exactly friendly way.

"One member of the Gang of Old Smelly Men down, and the worst one of 'em as far as I'm concerned. Hell, he was irritating enough that I wouldn't be surprised if one of the others turned him in. Whoever it was knew enough about the robbery to point the cops toward the rest of the loot."

"Including that gold record everyone was so het up about," Mark added. "However the good Widow O'Quinn feels about this town, and especially about her family, she was right glad to know it was all back safe. Enough so she's making another big donation once they expand the museum."

Tansy blinked, honestly surprised at this bit of news.

"Expansion? How'd that happen?"

Tim shrugged and held up his hands, but he was grinning.

"Damnedest thing, but I have to say it makes sense. We never did get the bunch of big Nashville media coverage the cops were afraid of, but that crash was more than enough to get the word out to locals on a slow night. Turns out more people cared about Captain O'Quinn and the Confederates than anyone knew about."

Mark took his turn in the long-standing tag-team stream of chatter.

"Or maybe they learned about them for the first time. You know, kids getting into things their grandparents liked. Anyway, a bunch of donations flooded in, and sounds like they're going to get some new grants and maybe even state funding. You know how this corner of Virginia gets excited about grabbing any little bit of music history to show up Tennessee."

Tansy shook her head, trying not to smile herself. She wasn't about to admit it to the best chatterboxes she'd ever met, but she wouldn't bet against Lori Jane having a hand in that word getting out and helping the money roll in.

"I'll be damned," she said. "So they're mostly calling the whole thing wrapped up and solved?"

Tim tilted one hand from side to side.

"Mostly. Sounds to me like the department *wants* it all to be settled, know what I mean? Might be one or two who aren't lined up like they're supposed to be yet. But unless some big bunch of secret evidence turns up, that's probably how things will stay. Especially with both of the ones who might answer questions out of the picture."

Tansy snorted. "My auntie would say this was mean of me to say of the dead, and I guess it probably is. But I doubt either one of them has a line of defenders waiting to fight to clear their names. Vickie or Lee neither one ever hesitated to make an enemy every chance they got. Or to stab someone in the back."

The words snuck themselves out of her mouth before Tansy considered how they sounded, especially to herself. Thankfully Tim and Mark were too busy shaking their heads to notice if she turned a little green around the edges.

"Sure is a hard way to go through life," Mark said. "Got enough proof in my own mess of a family to prove that. Listen, anything you and Cat need before you set out? I know you've been busy on your visit and we have too, but it's been great to see you."

Tansy hesitated for a second, then darted forward to give Mark a quick one-armed hug. Before he could say a word, she did the same to Tim.

"Y'all are just saying that because things got so much more interesting around here when I showed up. Seriously, it's been great to see you, too."

Both men grinned and elbowed each other.

"Now I definitely want you to visit again," Tim said. "Before another big bunch of years slips by."

The lie came out easier than Tansy expected.

"I sure will. You two take care."

By the time she made it out the door with her chips and a few bottles of caffeine for the drive, Cat had both cars gassed up and ready.

"Your tires are in good shape, same thing under the hood. I reckon we're all set. Get everything sorted out in there?"

Tansy took a quick look around, glad she could barely catch sight of the Clinch River. Maybe not for the last time, but for the last time in a good while.

Probably a good thing with all the weird shit that had happened since Cat snuck up on her down at the picnic area her first day back.

If there ever was going to be a fresh start for either one of them, they better grab this chance while they had it.

"As sorted as it can be in this little town. I'll fill you in when we stop for lunch. Let's get moving and see what we can't get into further on down the road."

Cat grinned as she walked back to her own car.

"Kinda hate to tell you this, but knowing you and me, it's sure to be nothing but another great big pile of trouble."

Tansy snorted and shook her head, but she couldn't manage to disagree.

Trouble would surely go along for the ride when she and Cat were together.

And while she hoped things weren't *quite* so dramatic as they had been during her long-overdue homecoming, she was already looking forward to whatever happened next.

# ABOUT KARI

Kari Kilgore's wanderlust and imagination lead her all over the world on grand adventures. Her heart and family bring her home to her native Appalachian Mountains of Virginia. From that solid base and with the help of the ever-changing lens of her imagination, she brings those adventures to life in fiction.

She loves music, her friends, and driving, but she prefers to keep the drama on the page.

Kari writes romance, fantasy, contemporary fiction, mystery, and science fiction, and she's happiest when she surprises herself. She lives in the middle of the woods with her husband Jason A. Adams, various house critters, and wildlife they're better off not knowing more about.

## The Confidential Adventure Club

For Kari's exclusive free After The End stories and deleted scenes, discounts, early pre-sale releases, adorable pet photos, and a whole lot more not available anywhere else, join us in The Club.

Hope to see you there!

www.KariKilgore.com

www.SpiralPublishing.net
www.ConfidentialAdventureClub.com

# ALSO BY KARI KILGORE

I hope you enjoyed reading *The Great Gold Record Heist* as much as I enjoyed writing it.

To dive into more tales of mystery and crime, investigate www.KariKilgore.com/Mystery. If you're craving more adventures from the Appalachian Mountains, and in many genres, head over to www.KariKilgore.com/TalesFromAppalachia.

For more novels, novellas, and short stories where speculative elements are either slight or not there at all, pay a visit to to www.KariKilgore.com/ContemporaryFiction.

Be the first to know about release dates and check out more of my fiction, including almost every genre with plenty of romantic elements, at www.KariKilgore.com.

## The Storms of Future Past Series:

*Dreaming the Storm*

*Joining the Storm*

*Into the Storm*

*Fighting the Storm*

*Sensing the Storm: A Storms of Future Past Prequel*

*Storms of the Heart: A Storms of Future Past Romance*

*Storms of Future Past Books One through Four Collection*

**The Odd Society:**

*Independent by Means of Magic*

*Protected by Means of Magic*

**The Voices through Time Series:**

*Songs in the Mountain*

*Secrets in the Land*

*Sorrows in the Earth*

*Walking the Ghosts: A Voices through Time Novella*

**Dispatches from the Galaxy Stories:**

*Restricted Species*

*The Becalmed*

*The Garbage Belt*

*Plurapod Pathogen*

*The Changes Cascade*

**Novels:**

*Until Death*

*The Dream Thief*

*Hand Me Downs*

*Protecting Her Own*

*The Coffee Bomb and the Corporate Spy*

**Novellas:**

*Legacy of the Land*

*In the Pines*

*DNA Never Lies*

*The Box of Possibilities*

*Murder at the Fabulous Feline Emporium*

**Collections:**

*Fantastic Women: A Dark Fantasy Novella Trio*

*Fantastic Shorts: Volume 1*

*Near Future Forward (with Jason A. Adams)*

*Fantastic Shorts: Volume 2*

*Partners in Romance (with Jason A. Adams)*

*Dispatches from the Galaxy: A Space Opera Novella Trio*

*Fantastic Shorts: Volume 3*

*Escape into Romance: A Collection of Sweet Beginnings*

*Stepping Out of Reality: Short Spells of Appalachian Magic*

*Facing Down Extraordinary: A Series of Ordinary Heroes*

*Hacking Cybercrime: Dana Sanderson Short Mysteries*

*Shadows Mountain Deep: Six Appalachian Crime Tales (with Jason A. Adams)*

*Investigations Beyond Belief: The Initial Adventures of Deb Powers: Otherworldly PI*

*Passages in the Real World: Six Stories of Life's Transitions*

*Fantastic Side Trips: Side Characters Take Center Stage*

*A Kaleidoscope of Cat Tales: Five Stories of Cats and People Who Love Them*

*A Tapestry of Holiday Tales: Winter Adventures from the Odds and Endings Bookstore*

*Uncommon Holidays: A Different Side of the Season (with Jason A.*

*Adams)*

*Aunties Among Us: Five Tales of Fabulous Women*

*Four-Legged Heroes: When Pets Rescue People*

*Partnership in Crime: Six Journeys to Justice (with Jason A. Adams)*